A REPORTER ROLAND BE

Easter Egg Hunt
Murder

RACHEL WOODS

BONZAI
M O O N

BonzaiMoon Books LLC
Houston, Texas
www.bonzaimoonbooks.com

This is a work of fiction. Names, characters, places and incidents either are the product of the authors' imaginations or are used fictitiously, and any resemblance to actual persons, living or dead, business establishments, events, or locales is entirely coincidental.

ISBN 978-1-943685-29-5 (Print)

ISBN 978-1-943685-30-1 (Large Print)

1

Roland "Beanie" Bean took a sip from the bottle of Felipe beer he'd been nursing for the past hour and stared at his cell phone.

One message.

But, not the message he'd been waiting for since yesterday.

Beanie cursed under his breath and glanced over his shoulder at his wife, Noelle, beautiful in a pale-yellow sundress, the outfit she'd changed into after Easter services at church that morning. Laughing, Noelle nodded as she conversed with several other couples clustered on the multi-leveled flagstone terrace.

Though the conversation was engaging, Beanie found it hard to participate as he surreptitiously tried to check his cell phone, which he'd switched to vibrate mode. He'd been clutching the phone when he felt the device tremble. Anxious to check the message, he'd been trying to think of a good reason to excuse himself from the group when he saw his four-year-old Ethan tearing into a flower bed beneath a large mango tree.

He'd interrupted the conversation to explain that he wanted to make sure Ethan didn't destroy the yard. Noelle had given him a narrowed side-eye, but she hadn't tried to stop him. Beanie suspected she knew what he was up to, though.

Standing beneath the shade of the broad, leafy tree, protected from strong mid-afternoon sunrays, Beanie pocketed the phone and focused on his son. Ethan attacked the flower mound like a dervish, raking dirt with reckless abandon, determined to unearth another hidden Easter egg.

"Careful, bud," Beanie said, a gentle caution in his tone. "Don't pull up the flowers."

"Sorry, Daddy," said Ethan, giving him a toothless grin as he yanked a pink begonia from the dirt.

"It's okay, bud," said Beanie, reaching down to muss his son's springy curls. As Ethan continued his assault on the flower mound, scrambling around, soiling the knees of his tan pants, Beanie smiled to himself. He probably shouldn't have allowed Ethan to be so wild and rambunctious, but Beanie didn't want to be a disciplinarian when his son was having so much fun. Beanie had wondered if his boys—two-year-old Evan, also at the egg hunt being supervised by Noelle's mom—would be shy about playing with kids they didn't know.

For the past two years following Easter service, they'd taken the boys to an egg hunt at the park in their neighborhood, Oyster Farms, which was sponsored by the Home Owner's Association.

This year, Noelle had other plans for them.

The president of St. Killian University, where Noelle had a position as an adjunct professor, had invited their family to the annual Easter egg hunt he held at his home in Avalon Estates, an enclave of wealthy ex-pats, executives, and other professionals.

Noelle had told him the boys would be fine. His wife had been right. Their gregarious kiddos had no problems socializing and had already made new friends. Beanie glanced toward the terrace. Noelle, drinking a mimosa and mingling with the adults, seemed to be making new friends, as well. The networking was necessary for his wife's ambitions. She'd accepted the egg hunt invitation because she hoped to be considered for a full-time position as a professor at the university. Schmoozing with the people who could help her career was necessary for her goals. At the moment, Noelle was, once again, conversing with the university president, Ted Zamora, and his wife, Anna.

Beanie focused on the couple.

A St. Killian native, Ted had left the island to study international business abroad. Somewhere along the way, during his travels and throughout his career as an oil executive, he'd picked up a wife, who was from Ireland. A redhead, blue-eyed beauty, Anna spoke with a jaunty Irish brogue and co-owned an upscale clothing boutique that catered to the well-traveled rich and fabulous.

Next to the president and his wife were Ernie and Victoria DuVert. Ernie, a handsome Casanova type, was known for wheeling and dealing with other people's money. Most of the time, those other people were his wives. Victoria was the fourth Mrs. Ernie DuVert. Beanie had gone to high school with Victoria, a good-looking girl from the Dominican Republic, and recalled that she'd married an old rich guy when she was eighteen. He died a year later and left her his fortune, much to the chagrin of his grown children who were largely cut out of the will. They accused Victoria of marrying their father for his money, then tricking him into changing his will before she killed him with vigorous, acrobatic sex. He'd had a massive heart attack while they were making love, if Beanie remembered correctly.

Dr. Roger Pinkerton and his wife, Delaney, stood slightly behind the DuVerts. A pompous cardiologist with a raging God-complex, Roger was another former school mate. Delaney, a recovering alcoholic with mental issues, was soft-spoken and considered somewhat spineless. The couple was considered perfect for each other because Roger was controlling and Delaney was needy. She leaned on Roger, looking to him for direction and guidance. Roger, who was rumored to view his wife's problems with alcohol as a moral failure, nevertheless took pleasure in dominating his wife, whose subservience fed his over-inflated ego.

To the right of the Pinkertons and directly in front of Ted and Anna were Bob and Belinda Davenport. A stay-at-home-dad, Bob had spent most of the afternoon fussing about their three girls, dressed like fluffy bunnies. Earlier, the girls had jumped around, leading the kids and little ones into the Bunny Hop Dance. Belinda, a designer, and seamstress, was Anna's business partner and co-owner of the boutique. Glamorous and stylish, Belinda had the jaded disposition of a pampered fashionista, complete with a designer vape pen.

"Look, daddy!" Ethan held up the blue egg with triumphant glee. "I found it!"

"Good job!" said Beanie, giving his son a high five followed by an exploding fist bump. "How many do you have now?"

"Seven!" announced Ethan, proud of his accomplishment as he held up his Easter basket. "But, I have to find more eggs! I want the most eggs!"

Ethan ran off, laughing and yelling as he joined the dozens of other children frolicking and skipping across the massive lawn behind the mansion. Bordered on the right by a grove of mature Hibiscus bushes and on the left by a fragrant lemon orchard, the yard was twice the size of the park in Oyster Farms and featured intricate landscaping perfect for hiding eggs.

Beanie checked his phone again. Still no new messages. Disappointed, he wandered back to Noelle, rejoining the circle of couples.

"What did I miss?" he asked Noelle.

"Anna cut her hand," said Noelle, sotto voce.

"I don't understand," said Belinda, blowing a stream of smoke from the side of her mouth. "Why were you cutting pineapple?"

"Don't you have a caterer?" asked Victoria.

Anna shrugged and looked away.

"I wonder if money is tight?" The question was a whisper on Beanie's left. Startled, he turned his head slightly. Chuck Taylor, who seemed to have appeared out of nowhere, gave him a sly smile. Beanie groaned inwardly. He wasn't in the mood for Chuck, or his wife, Florence.

Beanie had barely gotten away from them an hour ago when he'd encountered the worldly, globe-trotting couple at the hors d'oeuvre table.

Beanie had been grabbing another small bowl of ceviche for Noelle when the Taylors introduced themselves. Five minutes into the conversation and Beanie had them pegged as cosmopolitan, well-traveled, and gossipy. Beanie suspected they were the types to offer sympathy and compassion while secretly delighting in the failure of others.

"I heard the boutique isn't doing so well," continued Chuck. "Apparently, sales have taken a drive right off the proverbial cliff, and no one knows why. Anna blames Belinda and Belinda blames Anna. But, who knows?"

Or cares, thought Beanie, but he didn't express his apathy. A failing boutique he couldn't afford to shop at wasn't on his radar at the moment. He was more worried about the message he was waiting for.

Moments later, the group began to disperse as several different conversation threads formed. Victoria, Noelle, and Bob huddled together. Ted and Dr. Roger paired off. Delaney, Belinda, and Florence formed a trio.

Excusing himself from Chuck, Beanie walked toward a bench on the far-right corner of the terrace. Taking a seat, he checked his phone. Finally, the message he'd been waiting for. Relieved, Beanie sent a response, then waited.

Glancing up, he scanned the lawn for his kids. Ethan was still running around like the Tasmanian Devil. Noelle's mom, who was carrying Evan even though he could walk, stood at the edge of the orchard, pointing at the large, yellow lemons hanging from the tree.

Shifting his focus back to the couples, Beanie spotted Anna and Ernie at the far-left corner of the terrace. With aggressive gestures, Anna shook her head as she spoke. Ernie stood stiffly, arms crossed, and head cocked.

Beanie's phone buzzed. He checked the text. As the tension left his body, he sent a second response, thankful his plans were working out.

"What do you think that's about?"

Beanie glanced up. Chuck Taylor, holding a bottle of Felipe beer, stood in front of him, a hint of mischief in his wry smile.

"What is what about?" asked Beanie, standing.

Chuck used the beer bottle to point toward the far-left corner of the terrace. "Ernie and Anna. Seems like a heated discussion."

"Maybe," said Beanie, wishing he had a beer.

"You heard the rumors about them, right?" asked Chuck, taking a swig of the official beer of the Palmchat Islands.

Beanie shook his head, curious about Chuck's comment as Ernie nodded and held up a hand in front of Anna, which she pushed away. Glancing toward the center of the terrace, where most of the guests congregated, Beanie searched for Ted. Was the university president aware that his wife and Ernie, the Lothario who collected wealthy wives, appeared to be arguing?

"Bow chicka bow bow," said Chuck, adding a few lusty, bed-creaking sound effects.

Beanie stared at Chuck. "Are you serious?"

Lifting a shoulder, Chuck said, "What I hear anyway."

The journalist in Beanie demanded corroboration for rumors and allegations, but he was trying to get away from Chuck, not engage the man in further conversation.

"Look at that," said Chuck, his tone full of malicious excitement.

"What?" asked Beanie.

"Anna and Ernie are going into the house," said Chuck.

His curiosity growing, Beanie frowned. As Chuck had pointed out, Anna and Ernie were heading up the flagstone path that led from the terrace to the French doors that formed a wall enclosing the sunroom.

"Those rumors just might be facts, my man," said Chuck. "Bow chicka bow bow."

Not willing to entertain unfounded speculation, Beanie clapped Chuck on the shoulder. "That beer looks great. Think I'll get one."

2

Keeping an eye on Ethan, who'd just crawled under a stone bench in his quest to find his tenth egg, Beanie glanced toward the lemon orchard, looking for Noelle's mom and Evan.

The spot occupied by his mother-in-law and youngest son half an hour ago was now taken by Belinda and Bob. The stay-at-home dad and the stylish designer both gestured wildly, pointing fingers at each other. Beanie scratched his chin. First Anna and Ernie. Now Belinda and Bob were beefing.

"What do you think that's about?"

Irritated by the sound of Chuck's voice, Beanie suppressed an exhale and turned.

"Looks like Bob and Belinda are getting into it about something," said Chuck, his voice filled with malicious glee.

"I wouldn't know," said Beanie, turning his attention back to Ethan, still looking for hidden eggs.

"I know he's crazy for pissing her off," said Chuck. "She might look like she just stepped off the runway, but she's from the streets. What they call a 'Handweg Ho.'"

Beanie glared at Chuck. He knew the derisive, derogatory term used to marginalize and malign young women from Handweg, a tough, violent neighborhood few escaped, or survived. The term was especially offensive to Beanie because it had been used to describe his wife. Noelle had grown up in Handweg, but she'd beat all the odds that had been stacked against her. Still, there were people who didn't respect her, or think she deserved the success she'd earned, because of her background.

"Did you know she used to be in the PC-5?" asked Chuck.

Beanie bristled at the mention of the notorious island cartel responsible for most of the crime and violence across the Palmchat Island chain.

"Couldn't believe it when Bob told me," said Chuck.

Remaining quiet, Beanie stared toward Bob and Belinda. Their gestures weren't so wild anymore, but they stood rigid, as though they were each struggling to contain rage.

"You just never know about people, do you?"

Shaking his head, Beanie said, "No, you never do."

The boutique owner's ties to the island gang didn't surprise Beanie. He knew from experience that a successful, enterprising, beautiful, well put together woman could easily hide the secrets of her past.

"Ouch!" squealed Ethan.

Worried for his son, Beanie dropped to one knee in the grass to help Ethan maneuver from beneath the bench.

"You okay, bud?" asked Beanie, picking Ethan up as he stood.

Lower lip quivering, Ethan said, "The bench hit my head, daddy!"

Beanie held in his laugh as he walked toward the terrace, heading for the bench where Noelle sat talking to Anna, the university president's wife who co-owned the upscale boutique with Belinda. Ethan was at an age where nothing was his fault. None of the bumps or bruises he sustained were ever the result of his own roughhousing.

Moments later, Beanie joined Anna and Noelle. Her expression pained, Noelle held out her arms, reaching for Ethan. The little guy scrambled onto his mother's lap and laid his head on her shoulder.

"What happened?" Noelle asked Beanie.

"Just bumped his head," said Beanie.

"Poor baby," said Anna, giving Ethan a sad smile.

"Bumped his head?" Noelle's voice rose an octave. "Where? How?"

"He's okay," said Beanie, hoping Noelle wouldn't overreact and insist on taking their son to the emergency room. "Aren't you, bud?"

Staring at Noelle, Ethan said, "The bench hit me because I was looking for the eggs it was hiding under it!"

Anna gave an exaggerated gasp. "The bench had no right to do that!"

Kissing Ethan's forehead, Noelle whispered words of comfort as she hugged their son.

"He's so adorable," said Anna, smiling at Beanie.

Grinning, Beanie mussed Ethan's hair. "We think so."

"And so is Evan," said Anna. "Where is he? I want to pinch his little cheeks before—"

"Where have you been?" A commanding voice boomed out behind Beanie.

Turning, Beanie frowned as Ted Zamora stalked toward them.

Stopping in front of his wife, Ted said, "I've been looking for you."

For a second, Anna scowled, but then her features softened, and she smiled. "Oh, I was just telling Beanie and Noelle that—"

"I need to talk to you," Ted insisted, then turned to Beanie. "I'm sorry. Please excuse us …"

Grabbing Anna's wrist, Ted pulled his wife to her feet, despite her small cry of protest.

Beanie glanced at Noelle as Ted took his wife by the elbow and steered her away. Noelle returned his confused, concerned look. As the couple walked away, Anna jerked her arm from Ted's grasp. Ted grabbed her arm again and pulled her along as he marched toward the house.

3

"Where have you been?" Chuck Taylor asked Ted when the university president returned to the terrace, joining the couples who'd been conversing, laughing, and opining about various topics.

The rest of the group glanced at Ted with barely disguised suspicion.

Discreetly, Beanie stepped behind Noelle and checked the time on his phone. Nearly an hour had passed since Ted had grabbed Anna and dragged her into the house. Beanie was still curious about why Ted had been so aggressive with his wife. Why had he insisted on pulling her away from the party to talk? The reporter in Beanie wanted answers. He and Noelle had engaged in mild speculation, but lacking facts, they'd abandoned coming to any conclusions.

"Where is Anna?" asked Florence.

Rubbing his chin, Ted said, "She's fine. She has a migraine and wanted to lay down."

"So, you realized that pink wasn't your color?" quipped Chuck.

Ted glared at him. "What?"

"You changed your shirt," pointed out Florence.

Ted's gaze shifted left and then right before he focused on the group again. Shrugging, he said, "I spilled beer on it."

Staring at Ted's light blue short-sleeved polo, Beanie realized he couldn't recall the color of the shirt Ted had been wearing when he'd led Anna into the house. Had it been pink? Beanie hadn't paid attention. It hadn't mattered.

"When?" challenged Florence.

Ted scowled. "Excuse me?"

"When did you spill beer on your shirt?" Chuck asked, the familiar malicious glee in his tone.

"What does that matter, Chuck?" Victoria asked, flipping a column of long, black hair over her shoulder. "I swear, you're such a donkey's ass sometimes."

"Donkey's ass," said Florence, tilting her head. "Isn't that redundant? Isn't a donkey considered to be an ass?"

Beanie suppressed a chuckle as Victoria rolled her eyes. His former classmate was still easily annoyed and didn't suffer those she considered fools.

Scoffing, Chuck said, "I'm an ass because I asked when he spilled beer on his shirt?"

"You're an ass because you always make a big deal out of nothing," said Victoria, tossing her hair again. "You always have."

"He always does," agreed Ernie, glaring at Chuck.

"I beg to differ," said Chuck, with amused indignation.

Rising from her chair, Delaney announced, "I'm going to check on Anna."

Roger grabbed his wife's arm, halting her progress. "Ted said she's fine. Let her rest. You don't need to—"

"I want to check on Anna," insisted Delaney, her voice shrill as she jerked free of her cardiologist husband. As Delaney hurried toward the flagstone path leading to the wall of French doors, she stumbled slightly. Beanie hoped the recovering alcoholic hadn't fallen off the wagon.

Blowing smoke after a long drag on her vape pen, Belinda stood and said, "I'll go with you."

"Wait for me," said Victoria, following Belinda.

Grabbing Noelle's hand, Beanie led her away from the group, toward the bench in the far left corner of the terrace. As they sat down, Beanie put his arm around his wife. Noelle leaned her head on his shoulder.

Enjoying a moment of peace and quiet reflection, Beanie smiled as he focused on Ethan, recovered from his mishap with the stone bench, running and jumping. Still full of energy, Ethan grabbed the hand of his little brother, who toddled along, eager to keep up. Close by, Noelle's mom watched, laughing and making sure her grandsons played safely.

"This was a nice day, huh?" said Noelle.

"The boys have had a great time," Beanie said.

"What about you?" asked Noelle. "You're not upset that we came here instead of Oyster Farms park, are you?"

"No, why would you think that?" Beanie glanced at his wife.

Gazing at him, she said, "You seemed distracted when we first got here."

"I was," admitted Beanie, tilting his head to plant a kiss on his wife's nose. "Not because I didn't want to be here, but because I was waiting to hear back from a source I need for the story I have to file tomorrow."

"Did the source contact you?" asked Noelle.

Beanie nodded. "I'm free to relax and enjoy myself."

As his wife snuggled against him, Beanie pulled her closer, content as he gazed at the late afternoon sun slanting across the lawn. A moment later, he closed his eyes, allowing the lazy breeze to lull him.

"Belinda's back," said Noelle. "Wake up. I want to see how Anna's doing."

Blinking, Beanie sat up and rubbed his eyes. "Was I asleep?"

Giggling, Noelle said, "You were dozing a bit."

Shocked, Beanie asked, "For how long."

Noelle shrugged and stood. "Maybe half an hour, or so?"

"Half an hour?" Beanie rose to his feet.

His wife took his hand and said, "You needed a quick nap."

Still surprised that he'd slept for thirty minutes, Beanie followed

Noelle back to the center of the terrace, where the group clustered around Belinda.

Florence asked, "How is Anna?"

Belinda replied, "She doesn't want to be disturbed. We need to let her rest, and—"

"Where's Victoria?" demanded Ernie.

Glancing around, Belinda said, "I don't know. She said she was heading back outside once we made sure that Anna was resting comfortably."

"When did she leave to come back out?" Ernie asked.

"Fifteen, twenty minutes ago," said Belinda.

"Well, she didn't come back out here," said Ernie. "So, where is she?"

Ted said, "Maybe she went to check on the kids?"

Chuck said, "Or, maybe she—"

"What the hell?" Florence exclaimed. "Oh my God! Delaney!"

"What's going on?" Beanie asked.

"Something's wrong with Delaney." Belinda stood. "Where's Roger?"

"There!" said Ernie, pointing toward the lawn. Beanie frowned as the cardiologist hustled his four kids to a bench and motioned for them to sit down. Turning, Roger headed toward the orchard, his halting jog quickening to a run.

Belinda hurried toward the orchard. Chuck, Florence, and Ernie followed her.

Noelle turned to Beanie. "Come on," she said, hurrying after Ernie and the others. Beanie glanced at Ted. The university president looked concerned but made no effort to head toward the orchard. Curious about Ted's reluctance, Beanie took off across the lawn. He reached the lemon orchard as Delaney stumbled out of the trees and into the arms of her husband.

Whipping her head left and right, Delaney staggered back and forth as she babbled. Concerned and confused, Beanie wondered if the woman was having a mild stroke, or maybe a seizure. She looked crazed and disheveled. Her silky lavender top was ripped near the shoulder. There were bloody scratches on her cheek. Torn hibiscus petals and leaves were stuck in her hair.

"Delaney," said Dr. Roger, holding his wife at arms' length as he stared at her. "Calm down, sweetheart! You're okay … just focus and breathe!"

As Roger separated Delaney from the rest of the group, Beanie moved closer to Noelle and slipped his arm around her waist. "I wonder what happened?"

Noelle said, "I don't know. You don't think any of the kids saw her, do you?"

Beanie glanced over his shoulder. Oblivious, the children continued to run and scream and hop and dance and skip, still concentrated on playing with each other and finding more hidden Easter eggs.

"Kids are okay," said Beanie.

Ernie asked, "What was Delaney doing in the lemon orchard?"

"I thought she was still in the house with Anna," Belinda said.

"I hope she's okay," said Noelle.

"I hope she's not drinking again," said Ernie.

"I hope she's not going to stab someone again," quipped Chuck.

"That's not funny," snapped Belinda, glaring at Chuck.

"I'm not joking, I'm serious," said Chuck.

Florence said, "You know she's psychotic."

"Certifiably insane," said Chuck.

"Maybe she's off her meds," wondered Florence.

Shaking her head at Florence, Belinda walked away, following Roger as he guided Delaney back to the terrace.

"You two are horrible," said Ernie, glaring at the Taylors with disgust before he turned and walked away.

"This reminds me of the time when Delaney had that meltdown in the cafeteria," said Florence, glancing at Beanie. "This was back when we were in high school. St. Killian Prep."

Nodding, Chuck said, "She attacked a teacher with a plastic butter knife. Stabbed the poor woman in the eye."

"Then she fainted," said Florence. "When she woke up, she was disoriented and incoherent, with no memory of what she'd done …"

4

Two-year-old Evan whimpered, his little lower lip stuck out as he pulled his hand away from his grandmother's grasp and ran toward Beanie, sitting next to Noelle on a tree seat surrounding a large coconut tree.

"Careful, sweetie," cautioned Noelle, who jumped up and ran to meet their youngest little boy. Scooping him up in her arms, she planted kisses on his face as she walked back to the tree seat, followed by her mother.

When Noelle sat down, Evan climbed toward Beanie, who embraced him and kissed his forehead.

"What's the matter?" asked Noelle, wiping Evan's chubby cheek. "Mom, did he hurt himself?"

Noelle's mother sighed, looking lovingly at little Evan. "No, he just didn't find as many eggs as the other little children, but I told him that was okay."

"Oh no," said Noelle, a slight tremor in her voice.

Standing Evan on his knees, Beanie glanced at his wife. Not surprisingly, Noelle was near tears. His wife was a bit overprotective and was desperate to shield their sons from problems, but Beanie didn't want to raise their sons in a bubble. He would protect his boys with his life, but they had to learn that life wasn't always going to be easy or fair or free from problems and worries.

Not willing to have his son, and his wife, bawling about Easter eggs, Beanie said, "Want Daddy to help you find more eggs?"

"What a good idea, Evan!" Noelle smiled through her tears. "You and Daddy can hunt for eggs."

Evan's crumpled sad face disappeared as he smiled and laughed. "Daddy find eggs!"

Beanie's heart swelled and soared as his son clapped his hands and squealed in delight.

"Evan, Daddy, will help you find lots of eggs," said Noelle's mom.

"Come on, Daddy," said Evan, tapping his feet on Beanie's knees. "We find eggs! Let's go!"

Cheered by Evan's enthusiasm and Noelle's encouragement, Beanie stood with Evan in his arms. After waving goodbye to Noelle and her mom, father and son headed off to hunt.

Fifteen minutes later, after no luck finding any eggs, Beanie was beginning to wonder if Ethan had, in fact, found all the eggs. His oldest son's goal had been to find every hidden egg. Good thing was that Evan didn't seem discouraged. He ran around on his stubby legs, pointing under bushes and trees, suggesting places to look.

At present, they were in the Hibiscus grove. Evan had spotted a narrow path between two mature flowering bushes. "Daddy, that way!" he'd said, taking off in that direction. Beanie followed, keeping a close eye on the little guy. The Hibiscus grove was a maze of bushes and interconnecting pathways. Beanie didn't think any eggs had been hidden in the grove, but he would allow Evan to explore for awhile before he suggested they look elsewhere.

As Evan approached one of the large bushes, attracted by a butterfly perched on a leaf, Beanie paused to take a deep breath. The warm, fragrant breeze danced across his face, fluttering the hibiscus petals.

At once, his mind flashed back to Delaney Pinkerton.

There had been crushed Hibiscus petals in her disheveled hair.

Beanie frowned. Delaney had staggered out of the lemon orchard. So, what was she doing with hibiscus petals in her hair? Had she been in the Hibiscus grove?

"Butterfly, daddy!" Announced Evan, pointing to the insect. "Fly, butterfly!"

Evan's high-pitched laughter sent the butterfly flapping its wings, ascending into the air.

"Bye-bye, butterfly!" Evan waved, watching the butterfly as it flew to another bush on the opposite side of the path. "Where are you going butterfly?"

Beanie rubbed his chin, recalling Delaney's strange episode. Had she suffered some sort of medical issue? Or, the effects of substance abuse? Didn't matter. Beanie hoped the woman would be okay, for her own sake, and the sake of her four kids. Hopefully, Roger would get his wife the help she needed.

Roger, Delaney, and their four kids had decided to leave the egg hunt and head home. Initially, the kids had protested, considering that the sun hadn't set and there were at least two more hours of daylight, but Roger quieted them with stern words and a glacial glare. Delaney, silent and shell-shocked, clung to her husband as they left the back lawn.

Beanie stared at a Hibiscus flower on the bush next to him. Did one of the paths in the Hibiscus grove lead to the lemon orchard? Or, maybe—

His phone buzzed. Removing the cell from his pants pocket, he checked the message. Smiling, Beanie read the "Happy Easter" text from his sister, Robyn, a physician's assistant who worked at a health clinic in the neighboring island of St. Basil.

"C'mon, Daddy! Hurry, Daddy!" Evan called out, running down the path. "This way, Daddy!"

"Okay, wait for Daddy," said Beanie, responding to his sister's message. After pocketing his phone, he glanced toward the pathway.

Evan was gone.

Beanie suppressed the quick, initial burst of panic shooting through his veins. There was no need to worry or think the worse. His little tyke couldn't have gotten that far.

"Evan, where are you?" Beanie cried out, walking briskly along the path, scanning the bushes and trees, searching for places where Evan might be hiding. "Evan!"

Reaching a small clearing where the path forked, Beanie froze for a moment. Which way should he go? Left, or right? He wasn't sure. The panic returned, making it difficult to think.

"Evan!" Beanie ventured left, praying he'd made the right decision. "Evan, where—"

"Sleepy lady, Daddy ..."

Beanie felt a sharp tug on his pant leg and glanced down. Smiling, Evan stomped his feet against the ground. "Sleepy lady, daddy! Sleepy lady!"

Relieved to see his youngest son safe and sound, Beanie crouched down. "Evan, please don't run off from daddy again, okay?"

Sticking out his lower lip, Evan nodded, and looked contrite, but only for a moment. Seconds later, his face lit up with excitement as he said, "Sleepy lady, daddy!"

Grabbing Evan, Beanie stood, holding Evan in the crook of his arm. "Sleepy lady?" Beanie was confused. What was his little man talking about?

"Over there!" Evan pointed somewhere behind Beanie.

Turning, Beanie faced a wall of bushes. "Where is the sleepy lady?"

"I show you, daddy!" announced Evan, kicking his legs, a signal that he wanted to be allowed to walk.

Worried that Evan would run off again, Beanie tightened his hold on Evan, who squirmed. "Tell Daddy where to find the sleepy lady."

"There, daddy!"

Beanie turned. Two large bushes flanked a narrow pathway through which Beanie saw several more bushes.

"That way, daddy," instructed Evan, pointing toward the pathway.

Wary, Beanie took a few tentative steps down the path, careful to turn his body so that no wayward leaves or branches would accidentally scratch Evan. Sleepy lady? What could that mean? Had Evan seen someone sleeping in the Hibiscus grove?

His wariness turning to worry, Beanie exhaled as he continued, even though he wasn't sure he should. The father in him wanted to turn and get the hell out of the grove. A strange silence had settled among the fragrant bushes, interrupted by a slight breeze that rustled the branches. The afternoon sun shot between the trees, casting oddly-shaped shadows across the path.

"Over there, daddy," said Evan. "The sleepy lady."

Following his son's little finger, Beanie pivoted toward a bush to his left.

"Sleepy lady is under the tree, daddy."

Sleepy lady under the tree?

Beanie's gaze dropped to the base of the tree.

Jolted, he held in a curse as he clutched Evan tighter and stepped back, staring at the woman sprawled in the dirt beneath the bush.

The sleepy lady.

Only she wasn't sleeping.

Covering the crime beat in Handweg Gardens, Beanie had seen enough corpses to know when he was staring at a dead body.

Squinting, Beanie focused on the red hair.

The sleepy lady was Anna Zamora.

Sucking in a breath, Beanie turned, trying to prevent Evan from seeing the body while he surveyed the scene. What the hell had happened to Anna? Her bright red hair was matted to the back of her head. Beanie looked closer and saw a bloody gash. His suspicions confirmed, Beanie spun away from Anna's body, anxious to get Evan away from the dead woman. Had Anna fallen and hit her head somehow? That didn't make sense. Ted said she was resting, trying to get over a migraine. Had she wondered out of the house and … and what? Beanie didn't know, but there was no time for speculation right now. The reporter in him had to take a backseat to his role as a father.

He had to get Evan out of the Hibiscus grove and back to the egg hunt. Once his little man was safe in Noelle's arms, Beanie would call the police.

And he'd have to tell Ted that his wife was dead.

"Bye, bye, sleepy lady," said Evan, leaning his head on Beanie's shoulder. "Goodnight!"

5

"I'm worried that Evan saw a dead body," said Noelle.

Exhaling, Beanie stared at his beautiful wife, leaning against the counter next to the refrigerator, arms folded, her expression grave. Beanie took a sip of coffee, buying himself some time, taking a moment to think of the best way to respond. He had to be careful with his words.

Noelle was upset and heartbroken by Anna's death, but she was more disturbed that Evan had been present when Beanie discovered the boutique owner's body. Beanie didn't want to seem as though he was discounting Noelle's concerns. He didn't want to appear to make light of Noelle's fear, even though he thought his wife was over-reacting. Beanie took another sip of coffee and then took a deep breath. The lingering smell of eggs and goat sausage made him long for a second helping of the breakfast dish his wife made better than anyone.

Beanie wasn't about to tell Noelle that she was acting paranoid. He wasn't going to give her a reason to remind him that, as a mother, she automatically worried about the boys more than he did because she'd carried them in her womb. Beanie didn't think their levels of worry should be compared, or that his degree of concern didn't measure up or match his wife's, but he didn't want to argue.

Especially since he knew why Noelle was worried.

When she was a teenager, his wife had seen her share of corpses while living in Handweg, where she'd fallen prey to gang life.

"Evan didn't know she was dead," said Beanie, deciding to stick to the facts and keep his opinions about his wife's concerns to himself. "He thought she was asleep."

"Are you sure Evan didn't see any blood?" asked Noelle, apprehension etched across her delicate features as she rubbed her hands up and down her arms.

Beanie nodded. "I'm sure."

Noelle exhaled, shaking her head. "I can't believe Anna is dead. Can't believe someone murdered her."

Beanie couldn't believe they were still discussing the murder. Two days had passed since Beanie had found Anna's dead body in the Hibiscus bush. He wasn't as disturbed and shocked as he'd been when he'd grabbed Evan and hurried back to the terrace, navigating the paths that twisted and snaked through the Hibiscus trees, trying to remember which way to go even though all he could think about was Anna, lying dead under the bushes … the sleepy lady, his little guy had called her.

After the cops came out and cordoned off the yard, Detective Philippi Janvier had declared the house and grounds a crime scene. Guests were questioned, and statements were taken. After giving terse, one-word answers to Janvier, a man he still despised, Beanie had texted Vivian Thomas, the *Palmchat Gazette* Managing Editor, about the murder. Vivian had given Beanie the task of writing the story, which had appeared first on the paper's website as breaking news before appearing in the daily publication the next day on Monday.

Though Beanie had written the initial article, a basic who, what, when, where, why, just the facts piece, he hadn't expected to work on any follow-up pieces. He'd thought Vivian would assign the follow-up story to Stevie Bishop, who was being groomed to be an investigative reporter. But so much for his expectations. Yesterday afternoon, before she left the office to go home, Vivian had stopped by Beanie's desk to announce that she wanted him to continue his coverage of the story.

Shocked, Beanie had voiced his discontent, reminding his boss that he was immersed in another investigation, one she'd encouraged and supported.

"But you know these people," Vivian had said. "You have a unique perspective on this story that our readers will find fascinating. You didn't just witness the news. You were part of the news."

Beanie balked, but Vivian stood her ground.

Glancing at his wife, Beanie said, "I can't believe I have to write the story. The Egg Hunt murder. That's what the *Palmchat Gazette* has dubbed it."

"That's what Anna's death has been reduced to?" asked Noelle, frowning. "The Egg Hunt Murder?"

"Babe, you need a good hook to sell papers," said Beanie.

"Do the police have any suspects?" asked Noelle, joining him at the kitchen table. "What do you know?"

"Not much …"

"Haven't you talked to the cops? It's your story, right?"

"Yeah, that's the problem," said Beanie, contemplating a third cup of coffee.

Noelle asked, "What do you mean?"

"I didn't want this story," Beanie confessed. "Vivian should have given it to Stevie."

Frowning, Noelle asked, "Why don't you want the story?"

"Because I'm working on something more interesting right now and I want to stay focused on that," said Beanie. "I'm in the middle of a story that will be more impactful to many more people."

Her left eyebrow arched, Noelle asked, "You're working on a more interesting story? That's why you don't want to cover Anna's murder?"

"Not only that," said Beanie. "I just feel I'm beyond writing about a dead body found in a Hibiscus grove. I'm a better writer now. Anna's murder needs to be covered but it's a simple story, and I want to do complex investigations."

"It wasn't just a dead body under a tree, Roland," said Noelle. "It was a woman we know. My boss' wife. A woman I had gotten to know and like and respect. I can't imagine that your readers would be bored by a woman whose skull was split open."

Beanie asked, "Who told you Anna's head was split open?"

Noelle said, "I talked to Florence last night."

Beanie sighed, bothered by Noelle's conversation with the unrepentant gossip. Florence Taylor was the very last person Noelle should have been talking to about Anna's murder.

"That's not true." Beanie shook his head. "She had a gash on her head, but her skull wasn't cracked open. I was there, remember? I know what I saw. I told you what I saw."

"You said she was stabbed."

"She was," said Beanie.

"You didn't mention the head wound," said Noelle, an accusation in her tone, like maybe she thought he'd kept some detail from her on purpose.

Beanie said, "I'm sorry I didn't—"

"Did Evan see the gash on Anna's head?" asked Noelle. "Did he see any blood?"

"Don't worry, okay."

"How can I not worry?" Noelle glared at him. "Children are deeply affected by traumatic experiences. They can develop PTSD, and—"

"Elle, you have to calm down or Evan will pick up on your worry and your stress, and then—"

"I know that. I'm sorry. I just … " Noelle pinched the bridge of her nose. "I never wanted my kids to go through what I went through."

Beanie said, "I know …"

"No, Roland, you don't know," said Noelle. "There's so much that you really don't know."

Worried, Beanie asked, "What are you talking about? What is it that I don't know?"

Sighing, Noelle looked away.

Beanie waited, uneasiness threatening to overtake him, to lead him down a path of suspicion. Noelle had kept things before. Crucial things. Important things about her past. Things she should have told him, but she hadn't, and Beanie still wasn't sure why she couldn't trust him with the truth.

His wife glanced at him, and said, "I just don't want Evan to have nightmares."

"He's been sleeping fine."

Noelle said, "I know, but …"

She trailed off, her doubt and disbelief hanging over him, like a cloud, palpable, indicting him, making him feel like the world's worst dad, concerned with his big explosive story instead of his son's potential PTSD.

Noelle said, "Florence said the cops think they found the murder weapon last night. A knife with Anna's blood still on it. Is that true? Did you know that?"

Beanie had heard about the knife, a ten-inch butcher's blade discovered in the Hibiscus grove, a few feet from Anna's body, but he didn't have any details beyond what he'd picked up on the police scanner.

"I'm planning to talk to Officer Fields today," said Beanie, placing his empty coffee mug on the table. "Hopefully, he'll be able to give me more information."

Rising from the table, Noelle said, "Well, let me know, okay? I have to go, or I'm going to be late for work, and I still have to drop off the boys at my mom's."

After a kiss goodbye and wishes for a good day, Noelle left. Beanie walked to the Keurig machine, convinced he needed the third cup of coffee. As the machine dispensed his steaming brew, Beanie wondered if

Officer Fields would have any new developments in the Anna Zamora murder.

And he wondered about all the things he still didn't know about his wife, the things she didn't want to share with him.

Beanie worried that there were more secrets Noelle had yet to reveal.

6

"Remember I told you I didn't want to write the follow-up for the Egg Hunt Murder," groused Beanie, using the hands-free setting on his phone to converse with his sister Robyn as he drove from the *Palmchat Gazette* office toward Avalon Estates to meet with Ted Zamora. "Well, guess what? I got assigned to cover the story."

After checking in with Vivian at the paper, Beanie had met with Officer Damon Fields at the St. Killian police department. A former high school classmate, Fields was gregarious, good-natured, and could be counted on to give Beanie straight answers. Beanie was glad to avoid Detective Philippi Janvier, who prided himself on being as vague and evasive as possible. Beanie couldn't stand the guy. Detective Janvier had put Noelle through hell last year.

"Roland, stop complaining," suggested Robyn. "Just write the damn hell out of the story."

"I don't want to write the hell out of the Egg Hunt Murder," Beanie said, earning a finger and a blaring horn from a driver when he switched lanes. "I'm working on something else. Something important. Something big."

"Can you give me details?"

"Well, without revealing my sources," said Beanie, turning off the main highway, "let's just say that the PC-5 is going into politics … "

"The PC-5?" echoed Robyn, her voice hollow. "You're writing about the cartel?"

Signaling a lane change, Beanie reflected on the apprehension in his sister's tone, which wasn't surprising. The PC-5 was a dangerous island mafia known for its vast criminal empire, which spanned across the Caribbean.

"Are you sure writing about the PC-5 is a good idea?" Robyn asked.

"Why wouldn't exposing those bastards be a good idea?"

"Because those bastards are dangerous," said Robyn. "Those bastards won't hesitate to retaliate against you—or your family. You know better than anyone how they operate and if you've forgotten, just ask your wife."

Beanie exhaled. Noelle's past connection to the PC-5 was a sensitive, thorny topic with Robyn. His sister had been livid, and terrified, when Beanie had confided in her that his wife had once been in the cartel, working first as a thief and then as a low-level drug dealer.

"I'm well aware of how dangerous the PC-5 is," said Beanie. "But I can't just keep complaining and lamenting how bad the organization is, I have to do something. They say the pen is mightier than the sword."

"I don't want your pen to put you on the PC-5 death list," said Robyn.

Beanie said, "Those bastards are going to try to take over the Palmchat Islands. They are going to turn the islands into an unofficial de facto dictatorship. If they govern the islands, they can guarantee that their criminal enterprise becomes more powerful. They'll go forth, unchecked and untouchable. No one will be able to stop them. Not the cops or the legislature or the judiciary. If their plans succeed, and one of their leaders becomes Prime Minister, then the cartel will be in the perfect position to control every level of government. That's the story I need to be working on. That story has got to be told. People need to be warned before it's too late."

Robyn said, "The PC-5 should be exposed, but I don't think you should have to expose them. I would prefer you cover the Egg Hunt murder."

Beanie groaned. "You sound like Vivian."

"Maybe your editor doesn't want you to be killed," Robyn said before announcing that she had to get back to work.

After quick professions of love, Beanie ended the call and continued his drive.

Beanie understood why his sister was worried for him, but he wasn't going to be intimidated by thugs. He'd already talked to Vivian and Leo about the PC-5 prime minister story, and they had encouraged him to investigate.

Beanie was anxious to follow up on the leads he'd uncovered, but he couldn't do that if he was working the Egg Hunt Murder.

Turning off the main highway, Beanie followed the two-lane road, which curved around the side of the mountain. He approached a T-intersection and made a right onto a wide boulevard. Perfectly picturesque, the paved road featured well-maintained tropical landscaping – tall Queen palms, vibrant Oleander, and Hibiscus bushes, and rows of fruit trees – coconut, mango, guava, and lemon.

Rolling down the window, Beanie breathed in the fresh citrus scent.

The lemon trees took him back to the moment when Delaney Pinkerton came stumbling out of the orchard, rambling and disoriented. What could have happened to Delaney? Had she had too much to drink? Or a traumatic medical event? How was she doing now? Roger, Delaney and their four kids had left the Zamora mansion before Beanie had discovered Anna's body. Had Roger Pinkerton told his wife that Anna was dead? Or was Roger concerned that Delaney might become unhinged if she knew Anna had been stabbed to death?

Continuing along the palm-lined avenue, Beanie shifted his attention to the posh surroundings. He couldn't help wondering what it would be like to raise his boys in an exclusive community of luxury. He couldn't help wishing that he could move his family to Avalon Estates. But wishing wouldn't make it happen. He needed to do something to make it happen. He had to write complex, compelling stories that would make a global impact. He had to build his brand as an investigative reporter. He wanted to be known for hard-hitting, compelling, uncompromising journalism that made a difference.

Moments later, Beanie steered the SUV into the circular driveway of the Zamora mansion, a huge contemporary Colonial made of tan stucco with plantation shutters flanking large picture windows. Back at the scene of the crime, he thought, exiting the vehicle. Walking up the wide, flagstone path toward the ornate double-door vaulted entryway, Beanie reflected on his conversation with Officer Fields.

After confirming that the cops had found the murder weapon—a butcher's knife—Fields had confided that said knife had been discovered wrapped in an expensive dress shirt that belonged to Ted Zamora. The cops had brought the university president in for questioning last night. Ted had denied having anything to do with his wife's murder, but Detective Janvier didn't believe him. Beanie wasn't surprised. Quick to jump to unfounded conclusions and slow to examine the evidence critically, Janvier was the kind of detective who made up his mind about the killer and then took steps to prove his suspicions, despite the lack of clues.

Five minutes later, Beanie sat on one of the four couches grouped in a square around a large bamboo coffee table in the spacious living room.

Ted Zamora, holding a cut crystal tumbler of whiskey, alternated between pacing around the plush tufted divans and dropping down onto the cushions. Despite the liquid courage, the university president looked haggard and yet furtive. One moment, he seemed spurred by manic energy. The next, he appeared lethargic and disoriented, a stranger in his own home, unaware of his surroundings and unsure of himself.

Beanie had spent the first few moments thanking Ted for talking to him, considering that the man had spent all night in an interrogation room being berated by Detective Janvier.

"How are you holding up?" inquired Beanie.

"I'm not," said Ted, taking a sloppy gulp of the whiskey, which dribbled down the side of his mouth.

Beanie wasn't sure the liquor was a good idea, especially at eleven o'clock in the morning. But he wasn't about to judge the man's attempts to cope with his sudden, unexpected loss. Beanie had no idea what the hell he would do if anything ever happened to Noelle.

"So ... " Ted dropped down onto the couch across from Beanie. "I'm guessing this is not just a wellness check. You came to get a quote for your story, right? Came to find out if I'm going to be arrested for killing my wife?"

"Is that what the police think?" asked Beanie, though he already knew Detective Janvier's theory.

"Guess you know they found the murder weapon," said Ted, raising the glass level with his eyes. "One of our knives from the kitchen. Wrapped in one of my shirts."

"What do you know about that?" asked Beanie.

"I'll tell you what I told the police," said Ted. "All I know is my wife is dead. She was stabbed to death. But you already know that. You found her. As far as the knife wrapped in my shirt, I don't know. I can tell you that I didn't stab my wife and then wrap the knife in a shirt. I didn't kill Anna. I had no reason to."

"I want to ask you about something that happened at the egg hunt," Beanie said, recalling the moment when Ted had manhandled Anna into the house.

Finishing the whiskey, Ted leaned forward, put the glass on the coffee table, and then slouched back against the accent pillows.

Beanie said, "At one point, Anna was talking to me and my wife, and then you interrupted us. You were adamant about talking with Anna. The two of you went into the house, but then you returned to the party alone."

Frowning, Ted said, "Anna had a migraine. That's why she didn't come back to the party."

"What did you want to talk to Anna about?" asked Beanie.

Ted exhaled, running his hands through his thick, wavy hair. "We were arguing."

"About what?"

"Same old shit we always seemed to be arguing about for the past few months," said Ted, rubbing the patchy, thin stubble on his chin. "Then Anna did what she always did when she was tired of the conversation. She claimed I was giving her a migraine. So, I told her to lie down, get some rest. I told her I would go out and continue to entertain our guests."

"Why did you change your shirt?" asked Beanie, throwing the university president a curve-ball question.

"What?" Ted gave him a blank stare. "Oh, um … Anna had been drinking a Bloody Mary when we argued, and she threw the drink at me."

"Must have been a pretty intense argument," said Beanie, hoping Ted would slip up and reveal the reason for the disagreement with his wife.

Ted shrugged. "That's why I changed shirts."

"What about the shirt wrapped around the machete?" Beanie asked. "It belongs to you?"

Nodding, Ted said, "But it wasn't the shirt I was wearing at the egg hunt. And, as I said, the knife came from our kitchen, but the cops won't find my prints on that knife and not because I wiped them off. I didn't kill Anna."

"Do you have any idea who killed Anna?"

"I don't want my thoughts about that printed in your story," said Ted, his right eye twitching as he stared at Beanie.

"No problem," said Beanie. "Between me and you."

Leaning forward, Ted slurred, "Ernie DuVert."

Beanie was quick to hide his shock. "Why would Ernie want to kill Anna?"

"Ernie and my wife were having an affair," said Ted, leaning back against the couch, rubbing his eyes. "And Anna was going to tell Victoria … so Ernie killed her."

7

Three hours later, Beanie was in Ernie DuVert's spacious, glass-enclosed home office, sitting on the opposite side of a large antique desk, staring at the man Ted Zamora claimed was having an affair with Anna.

After a quick lunch hunched over his desk at the Palmchat Gazette, and an hour-long conference with Vivian about his conversation with Ted, Beanie had decided to contact Ernie, see if the guy would be willing to talk to him about Anna's murder.

Ernie had agreed but warned Beanie that he was in the middle of negotiations for a huge deal he'd brokered, and they might be interrupted from time to time.

"That's not gonna work," said Ernie, an iPhone pressed to his ear. "Because that's not what we initially agreed upon."

Moments ago, following mindless greetings and small talk, as Beanie sat down, Ernie's phone rang. A call he had to take, he claimed, whispering, "New York," before he answered the phone.

Beanie had nodded and glanced around the office, taking in the rich surroundings. The office was decorated in the classic, quintessential British Colonial style. Rattan furniture. Cane chairs. Natural fiber rugs.

Potted palm trees. Sepia-tinted maps of historic West Indian spice routes in mahogany frames.

Glancing at his watch, Beanie estimated that Ernie had been on the phone for fifteen minutes. Annoying, but the man had warned him. And the interruption gave Beanie a moment to contemplate how to question Ernie. Ted's allegations about Ernie killing Anna had surprised Beanie, but after his own reflections and his conversation with Vivian, he wasn't sure he believed Ted.

Following a brutal all-night interrogation with Detective Janvier, the man had no doubt been mentally exhausted and not thinking clearly. And he'd probably been drinking most of the morning. Beanie doubted he could trust Ted's alcohol-induced suspicions.

But if Ted's claims about Anna and Ernie were true, then Ted might have fingered Ernie out of spite.

Then again, Beanie remembered seeing Anna and Ernie arguing at the egg hunt. Could their heated discussion have been about Anna's threats to tell Victoria that Ernie was cheating? Possibly. Still, Beanie wasn't sure about Ted's admission.

"Horrible what happened to Anna," said Ernie. "Just terrible."

Jolted from his reverie, Beanie cleared his throat. "Very."

"So, you've talked to the police?" Ernie asked. "For your story?"

Beanie nodded.

Ernie leaned back in his chair and made a steeple with his fingers. "And what are they saying?"

"Not much," said Beanie. "Not to me at least."

"But, they brought Ted in for questioning," said Ernie. "That's what Florence Taylor told Victoria."

"Right," confirmed Beanie.

"So, the cops think Ted did it?"

Beanie stared at Ernie. Why was the man fishing for information? Was Ernie curious? Was he trying to find out if Ted was a suspect? Or was he trying to make sure that Ted was a suspect? If so, why? Maybe because if Ted was the prime suspect, then the police would suspend their search for the killer and he would be off the hook. Maybe. But, only if Ted had been right about his theory that Ernie had killed Anna.

Beanie said, "I'm not sure what the cops think."

"You think Ted will be arrested?"

"If there is evidence that he committed a crime," said Beanie, "then I don't see why he wouldn't be."

"Florence told Victoria that the cops found the murder weapon," said Ernie. "So, there is evidence. A knife with Anna's blood on it. Did the cops find Ted's prints on the knife?"

Beanie decided to change the direction of the conversation. "You knew Ted and Anna pretty well?"

Ernie stared at him. "Well enough."

"How did you meet?"

"Through Victoria," said Ernie. "She frequented the boutique Anna owned with Belinda. But we weren't best friends. The four of us went to dinner from time to time, and I played golf with Ted once or twice a month."

"Were Victoria and Anna friends?" asked Beanie.

"More like acquaintances," said Ernie.

"And what about you and Anna?" asked Beanie.

Eyes shrewd, Ernie stared at him. "What about me and Anna?"

"How would you categorize your relationship?"

"We didn't have a relationship," said Ernie.

Noticing that Ernie's gaze had shifted slightly to the left—an indicator of dishonesty—Beanie said, "I just asked because I saw you and Anna together at the egg hunt and you seemed to be having an intense conversation."

Arms crossed, Ernie said nothing.

Convinced that Ted had been telling the truth about Anna's affair with Ernie, Beanie said, "You looked like you were arguing."

Exhaling, Ernie rubbed his eyes, then stared at Beanie. "She was trying to blackmail me."

"Blackmail you?"

"Between you and me," said Ernie, "Anna and I were … involved … for a while."

"Involved," repeated Beanie. Interesting way to define cheating on your wife with another woman.

"Didn't last very long and it ended months ago," said Ernie, shrugging as he sat forward. "Wasn't serious, or anything. Wasn't the kind of situation where either of us was contemplating leaving our spouses."

"So Anna was threatening to tell Victoria about your affair?"

"Not sure if you're aware or not, but the boutique Anna owned with Belinda isn't doing very well," said Ernie. "Sales are down. Anna wanted me to invest in the boutique. A cash infusion, she called it."

"You refused?"

Scoffing, Ernie said, "I would have been throwing good money after bad. Neither Anna nor Belinda know how to run a business. Belinda's a great designer, sure, but Anna was just a bored housewife who wanted something to do besides lunching with the ladies and banging the pool boy."

"You were willing to risk Anna telling your wife about the affair?" asked Beanie.

Ernie said, "Anna and I were arguing because I was informing her that she had no leverage over me. She tells me to bail out the boutique, or she'll show Victoria a naughty video we made. I told her that Victoria already knew about the affair. She accused me of lying, trying to call her bluff, but it's true."

"How did Victoria find out?" asked Beanie.

Shaking his head, Ernie said, "I have no idea. Suffice it to say, Anna was pissed that she didn't have anything on me."

Beanie nodded slowly, giving himself a moment to process what Ernie had told him. If the man was being truthful, then he really had no motive to kill Anna. Ted's theory that Ernie had killed Anna was predicated upon the belief that Victoria didn't know about the affair. But, Victoria did know about the affair, according to Ernie. Was the man telling the truth? Had he and Anna argued about his refusal to help her failing business? Or had their heated discussion been about something else?

Standing, Beanie said, "Well, those are all the questions I have for now, so—"

"Before you go," said Ernie.

Beanie stared at Ernie, waiting, wondering what he wanted.

"Between you and me," said Ernie, his gaze intense. "Are the cops going to arrest Ted?"

"Why do I get the feeling that you want them to?" asked Beanie.

Ernie sighed. "Because when Victoria found out about my affair with Anna, she threatened Anna. I know you went to high school with Victoria. You know she has a temper, and she's territorial."

Beanie recalled Victoria as a tough, defensive girl prone to explode whenever she thought she was being slighted or disrespected. One of those kick ass first and take names later girls you didn't want to mess with.

"What do you mean she threatened Anna? How?"

Ernie said, "She told Anna to stay away from me, or she would kill her."

8

"Detective Janvier believes Ted killed Anna," said Beanie, leaning on the pillows propped against the headboard, staring at Noelle who was exiting the bathroom.

An hour ago, following dinner, they'd bathed the boys, read to them, and then put them to bed. Beanie enjoyed the nighttime ritual, even though Evan loved to splash water all over the place and Ethan never wanted to go to sleep. *One more story, pleeeeease*, Ethan would plead, and Noelle would give in. Three stories later, Ethan would finally drift off. Tonight had been no different—except for the fact that Beanie probably wouldn't be making love to his wife tonight.

His wife looked gorgeous in baggy pajama bottoms and a tank top. Beanie wanted to jump her bones, but Noelle was more interested in discussing the developments he'd found out about the Egg Hunt murder.

"Officer Fields doubts that Ted is guilty," said Beanie. "But the knife used to kill Anna was wrapped in one of Ted's shirts, so Janvier is convinced that Ted murdered his wife."

Rolling her eyes, Noelle shook her head. "I hate that Janvier is the detective assigned to investigate Anna's murder. Once again, he's rushed to judgment, jumped to the wrong conclusions. Ted would never kill Anna."

Beanie agreed with his wife's assessment of Janvier's detective skills, but the reporter in him questioned her belief in Ted Zamora's innocence. Noelle hadn't known Ted very long. He'd just been appointed to the position six months ago. How would she know whether the university president was capable of murder? Beanie suspected that his wife thought Ted was innocent because of her staunch belief in Detective Janvier's incompetence.

Beanie didn't blame his wife, after what Janvier put her through when he was investigating the murder of Eamon Taylor, a fellow pharmacist Noelle had been accused of killing. Despite the circumstantial evidence against his wife, Janvier had been convinced she'd murdered Eamon and had been hell-bent on proving his misguided theories.

Beanie said, "I'm not sure if Ted killed Anna, or not, but … he does have a motive."

Standing at the foot of the bed, Noelle stared at him. "A motive?"

"Anna cheated on Ted," Beanie said. "Did you know that?"

Noelle shook her head. "I had no idea."

"She had an affair with Ernie DuVert," said Beanie.

His wife's jaw dropped. "Are you serious? Victoria's husband? How do you know this?"

"Ted told me," said Beanie. "He also told me that he thinks Ernie killed Anna."

Gasping, Noelle climbed onto the king-sized bed. "Continue, please."

As his wife stretched out next to him, Beanie wrapped an arm around her and shared the details about his interviews with Ted and Ernie.

"You think Ted is right about Ernie killing Anna?" asked Noelle. "Or, is Ernie right about Victoria killing Anna?"

"Ernie doesn't really have a motive," said Beanie. "Anna tried to blackmail him, but it didn't work. She had nothing to hold over his head, so why would he kill her. As far as Victoria, she's a badass, and she probably did threaten Anna, but I don't know if she'd make good on that threat."

"Did you talk to Victoria?"

"Not yet," said Beanie. "But she's on my list. I want to talk to Belinda, too."

His wife tensed for a second. "Why do you want to talk to her?"

"She was Anna's business partner," said Beanie. "She might be able to confirm that Anna asked Ernie to bail out the boutique."

"Florence said the boutique isn't doing too good," said Noelle. "It caters to a very wealthy clientele, and those posh customers just aren't visiting the store as much as they used to."

"Chuck said Belinda used to be in the PC-5," said Beanie. "Is that true?"

Noelle nodded.

"Did you know her back then?" asked Beanie, though he knew his wife didn't like discussing her past with the island cartel.

"I knew of her," said Noelle. "But, we didn't hang with the same crew."

"Did you talk to Belinda at the egg hunt?" Beanie asked.

"I'm not sure. I don't remember," said Noelle. "But, you know who else should be on your list?"

"Who?" Beanie asked, deciding not to press Noelle about Belinda.

"Florence and Chuck."

"You're kidding, right?" Beanie scoffed. "Don't have time for their gossip and fake news."

"They have a lot of inside information about Ted and Anna, and Ernie and Victoria," said Noelle. "They know everything about everyone in Avalon Estates."

"I'll think about it," said Beanie, his mind wandering from Anna's murder to the subject he'd been thinking about off and on all day, a subject he knew Noelle didn't want to discuss.

After a moment's hesitation, Beanie said, "Speaking of people who know things …"

"Hmmm…" Noelle snuggled next to him.

"You know I'm working on the story about the PC-5."

Noelle tensed again. His wife wasn't happy about his decision to investigate the island cartel. She and his sister Robyn shared the same opinion, though they didn't know it because they barely spoke anymore.

"There's someone I need to talk to," said Beanie, still hesitating, not sure how to articulate a request he knew Noelle would refuse. "Someone who knows a lot about the cartel, and—"

"Someone like who?" asked Noelle, pushing away from him and sitting up.

Beanie exhaled. "Your dad."

"Are you serious? My dad?" Noelle scooted off the bed and glared at Beanie. "You want to talk to my father? I don't understand. Why would you want to talk to him?"

"I need a source who knows about the cartel for my story—"

"You mean the PC-5 story you shouldn't be writing?"

Beanie sighed. "Babe let me explain—"

"You can't talk to my father," said Noelle, shaking her head. "No. You just can't. Find someone else, if you insist on writing the story, but it can't be my dad."

Beanie struggled to temper his frustration at his wife's stubbornness. "Noelle, I just want to ask him—"

"I do not want you talking to my father," said Noelle, glowering at him. "I mean it, Roland. Do not go behind my back and—"

"Noelle, calm down, please," said Beanie. "I'm not trying to upset you, okay? I just wanted to see if you'd be willing to find out if your dad would talk to me, but I'm sorry I brought it up."

"Why would you bring it up?" asked Noelle. "You know I haven't spoken to my father in fifteen years!"

"I know you don't want to talk to your father—"

"I can't talk to my father," said Noelle.

Sitting forward, Beanie asked, "What do you mean you can't talk to him?"

Noelle exhaled and pinched the bridge of her nose. "I know you won't understand this, Beanie, but ..."

"But what?"

Wrapping her arms around herself, Noelle paced from the bed to the dresser, where she stopped and stared at herself in the mirror.

Worried about his wife, Beanie jumped off the bed and walked toward her. "Babe—"

Loud, sustained beeping interrupted his progress.

"Your phone," said Noelle, her voice flat.

"Forget the phone." Beanie walked to her and turned her around to face him. "Sweetheart tell me—"

The phone beeped again, the signal for an incoming text message.

"Might be important."

"Nothing is more important than you," Beanie told her.

Noelle sighed. "I'll be fine, okay? I'm going to get some water and check on the boys. I'll be back."

Beanie's shoulders slumped as he watched his wife leave the bedroom. He was pissed at himself for upsetting her, for causing emotional distance between them. He'd known it would be a mistake to ask Noelle to facilitate a meeting between him and her father, but he'd convinced himself that he could make his wife understand his position. He'd assumed she'd be willing to help him.

What the hell had he been thinking? Obviously, not about his wife's feelings. What he didn't understand was why his wife claimed she *couldn't* talk to her father. Did she mean that she was physically or emotionally unable? Or, had she been banned from talking to Josue Chartres, the notorious PC-5 enforcer of the cartel's horrific Death List.

The phone beeped again.

Annoyed, Beanie cursed and grabbed the phone from the bedtable, where he stored it on a charging dock station. The text was from Roger Pinkerton. Beanie frowned, reading the cardiologist's message.

Please call me ASAP. Extremely urgent.

"What the hell?" Beanie muttered.

The time displayed on his phone was 10:39 pm. Why was Roger contacting him so late? What could he want? What was so urgent?

Plopping down onto the bed, not in the mood, Beanie nevertheless returned the doctor's call.

"Roland, thank you for calling me back," said Roger, breathless. "I'm sorry to bother you."

"What's going on?" asked Beanie, anxious to find out what Roger wanted so he could get back to what really mattered—Noelle.

Roger Pinkerton said, "Delaney has been arrested."

Confused, Beanie asked, "Arrested? For what?"

After a long exhale, Roger said, "The murder of Anna Zamora."

9

"I want you to help me clear Delaney's name," said Roger Pinkerton, moments after welcoming Beanie into his spacious home on the corner lot of a cul-de-sac.

Beanie stared at the cardiologist. "You want me to what?"

Flabbergasted, Beanie wondered if he'd heard the man correctly. Roger's frantic phone call last night was disturbing. Explaining that he was standing outside the St. Killian police department, Roger had given him the most pertinent details. The cops had arrested Delaney for the murder of Anna Zamora. His wife had been booked and now sat in a holding cell, where she would remain until she could be arraigned during a bail hearing the next morning. Detective Janvier claimed to have irrefutable evidence that connected Delaney to the crime, but he hadn't revealed how or why he now believed Delaney Pinkerton was guilty. Roger had apologized for bothering him, but he wanted to meet with Beanie the following day after Delaney was released from jail.

Following Roger's call, Beanie had shared the news with Noelle, who'd wandered back into the room with a glass of white wine. Shocked and confused, his wife couldn't imagine why the police thought Delaney had killed Anna and blamed Janvier's ignorant incompetence.

Beanie had reminded Noelle that Delaney had hibiscus petals tangled in her hair when she'd stumbled from the lemon orchard.

Rolling her eyes, Noelle had said, "That just means she was in the Hibiscus grove at some point. Doesn't mean she killed Anna."

"Anna's body was found in the Hibiscus grove," pointed out Beanie, purposely leaving out that he—and Evan—had stumbled upon the corpse.

Noelle stared at him. "So?"

Beanie let it drop, deciding that his wife was still pissed at his request to talk to her father, and he shifted his speculation to why Roger Pinkerton wanted to meet with him.

"Maybe he wants the name of a good attorney," suggested Noelle. "You have to recommend Octavia Constant."

For his meeting with Roger—which was later in the afternoon than they had originally planned due to delays at Delaney's arraignment—Beanie had brought the business card of Octavia Constant, the Harvard-trained defense attorney he'd hired to represent Noelle when she'd been accused of murdering her co-worker.

When Beanie handed the business card to Roger, the cardiologist surprised him by admitting that he'd already hired Attorney Constant.

"I don't understand," Beanie had said. "If you don't want a recommendation for a good attorney, then what—"

Roger Pinkerton had revealed his true motives at that moment.

I want you to help clear Delaney's name.

"I know it's a lot to ask," said Roger. "And I know you have no reason to help me. I mean, sure, we went to high school together, but let's face it. We knew each other, but we weren't friends."

"Then why are you asking me to help you?"

Roger sighed, indicating that Beanie should follow him out of the spacious foyer, and into a large living area.

Beanie glanced around. The décor could have been described as luxury at its most sterile—cold and uninviting, mostly white and very neat and clean, with everything in order, nothing out of place, nothing askance or askew.

The furniture was modern, featuring boxy pieces that Beanie wasn't quite sure how to sit on, or if he was even allowed to. Odd for a couple with four kids, Beanie thought. Then again, the Pinkerton children were rigidly obedient and disturbingly polite and respectful. At the egg hunt, Beanie remembered being astonished that the quartet had managed not to soil their Easter outfits. Their search for eggs had been methodical and deliberate, the four of them working together as a collective unit.

Roger invited Beanie to sit with him on a leather sectional the color of fresh snow.

"Octavia Constant suggested that I call you."

"She did?" Beanie was surprised.

"When she took Delaney's case—I couldn't meet with you earlier because Delaney and I were meeting with Octavia—she said we could win if we found a better suspect," said Roger.

Remembering the lawyer's sage advice, Beanie said, "That's sort of her thing."

Nodding, Roger said, "She mentioned that you had been able to find a better suspect when Noelle was wrongfully accused of murder. That's why I called you. I'm a cardiologist. I can put a stint in your chest with my eyes closed, but I have no idea how to find a better suspect. I don't even know where to start. But you do. You're a reporter. You know how to investigate—"

"Octavia already has an investigator on her team," said Beanie. "Her cousin Icarus—"

"He doesn't work for her anymore," said Roger, waving a dismissive hand. "He can't help me, but you can."

"I don't know if I should get involved," said Beanie, pissed that Octavia had encouraged Roger to request his help. He appreciated everything the attorney had done for Noelle, but he didn't work for her, and he wasn't about to start. If her cousin had quit, then Octavia needed to hire a new investigator to search for better suspects.

"You're already involved," said Roger. "You're covering the story for the *Palmchat Gazette*. The Egg Hunt murder. Isn't it your job to interview me and Delany for your article?"

"An interview is different from an investigation," said Beanie, thinking of his story about the PC-5's efforts to control Palmchat Island politics. He didn't have time to find another suspect. He was in the middle of his own investigation. It was going well, but it would be better if he had a response from the cartel to the allegations in his story. Beanie had hoped Noelle's father could use the influence he'd had with the cartel to get Beanie a meeting with one of the five leaders. Didn't matter which one. Didn't matter if all Beanie got was "no comment" when he questioned them. His piece would be legitimized by an interview with a PC-5 leader.

"If I can't figure out who really killed Anna," Roger said, "then Delaney could go to jail for the rest of her life. Detective Janvier is convinced that she's guilty and won't even consider that someone else may have wanted Anna dead."

"I know all about that asshole Janvier," said Beanie, remembering what the detective had put his wife through. Roger was right about Janvier, Beanie knew. The man believed he was a great detective, and wouldn't entertain any other ideas or theories other than his own, whether they made sense, or not. "He tried to railroad Noelle."

"But he didn't. You stopped him," said Roger. "And I know it was because Noelle is your wife."

"Noelle is my life," Beanie corrected the cardiologist. "I couldn't let Janvier's bullshit investigation take her away from me."

"I feel the same way about Delaney. She means the world to me," Roger said. "That's the only reason I'm asking you to help me. It's a bold request, but I have the unmitigated gall to make it because I can't bear the idea of my wife and the mother of my children going to jail for something she didn't do."

Staring at Roger Pinkerton, Beanie recognized himself—the man he'd been when Noelle was accused of a vicious murder there was no way she could have committed. Like Roger, he'd been broken and desperate, willing to do whatever it took to clear his wife's name.

"I'll see what I can do," said Beanie.

10

"You should talk to Delaney," said Roger, as though giving a recommendation, something Beanie should do for his own good. "Her memory of the egg hunt is fuzzy, but maybe what she tells you can help your investigation."

Beanie nodded.

"She's in the library," said Roger, standing. "This way ..."

Library? Beanie was confused until he remembered that most homes in Avalon Estates had extra bedrooms, which homeowners often repurposed, turning them into yoga rooms, dance studios, playrooms, and even libraries.

After walking down a long wide hallway, they made a left onto another long wide hallway, and then a right down yet another long wide hallway. Disoriented, for a moment, Beanie feared he wouldn't be able to find his way out of the Pinkerton maze if he had to make a run for it.

In the library, Delaney stood with her back to them, facing a wall of ceiling-to-floor glass windows looking out to a large backyard with lush tropical landscaping surrounding a pool.

"Sweetheart ..."

Delaney turned, pulling her shawl tighter around her slumped shoulders. Her face was ashen, cheeks hollowed, eyes red-rimmed and haunted. She smiled, but Beanie suspected it was a struggle.

"Roland stopped by," said Roger. "Remember, I told you he was coming to ask you a few questions."

"Oh, yes, I remember," said Delaney. "How are you, Roland?"

"I'm doing well," said Beanie. "How are you?"

"As well as can be expected, I suppose," said Delaney, her steps halting as she walked to Roger and placed her hand on his arm, leaning against him. "Just so very grateful to no longer be in jail. It was very unpleasant. I missed Roger and the children horribly."

"That's all behind you now, sweetheart," said Roger, his tone soothing and yet succinct, brooking no argument from his wife.

"I don't want to go back there," said Delaney, clutching her husband with trembling hands as she stared at him. "I can't go back—"

"You won't have to, sweetheart—"

"You don't know that," said Delaney, her voice rising, becoming shrill, almost hysterical. "The police arrested me. They think I killed Anna. They could put me on trial. A jury might find me—"

"Delaney, calm down," said Roger, the comfort absent from his voice as he guided his wife to a divan in the center of the room. "Sit. Now take a deep breath."

Beanie watched, struck by Roger's authoritative dominance over his wife, who seemed more than willing to submit to his commands. Like an obedient canine, Beanie couldn't help but think.

"Roland is going to ask you some questions about the day Anna was found dead at the egg hunt," said Roger, staring intently at his wife. "You will need to remain calm and focused so you can give him clear, concise answers. Do you understand?"

"I understand. I can be calm. I can give clear answers," said Delaney, as though she was reciting a mantra.

Roger looked at Beanie and nodded, indicating that Beanie should take a seat on the chair adjacent to the divan.

Feeling as though he'd just been given permission to speak, Beanie cleared his throat. "Delaney, why don't you tell me, what happened when you went to check on Anna? Do you remember that? You, Belinda, and Victoria—"

"You remember that, sweetheart," said Roger. "Tell Roland what happened."

Clutching her husband's forearm, Delaney said, "We went into the house to make sure that Anna was resting because she had a migraine. We wanted to see if there was anything she needed. Anything we could do for her."

Beanie nodded, remaining quiet as Delaney trailed off, willing to let her recount the events at her own pace. The woman seemed confused, her eyes darting back and forth.

"Go on," Roger prodded his wife.

Delaney sighed. "The three of us went into the house and into the master bedroom, but Anna wasn't there. So, we got worried, and we realized we needed to look for her. We were afraid maybe she had collapsed, or something. Anyway, they have a large home, and we decided to split up. I went upstairs, and Belinda and Victoria stayed downstairs. After I couldn't find Anna, I went downstairs, and I saw Belinda leaving. I asked her if she'd found Anna, and she said that Anna was in Ted's study. Belinda said Anna confided to her that she'd faked the migraine to end an argument with Ted."

"So, then Belinda went back outside?" asked Beanie, recalling the moment at the egg hunt when Noelle mentioned to him that Belinda had returned. He'd been shocked to learn he'd dozed for half an hour.

Delaney nodded. "I went into the study because I heard loud voices."

"Loud voices?"

"Yelling and cursing," said Delaney, clasping her hands together, rocking slightly. "Victoria and Anna were arguing. I tried to get them to stop, but Victoria told me to stay out of it. She was screaming at Anna, telling her to get off the computer. Victoria was upset about something Anna was looking at on the computer. Anna told Victoria to get away from her, but Victoria grabbed Anna and pulled her out of the chair.

Victoria said, *I told you to stay away from Ernie.* Victoria said she would kill Anna if she found out that Anna was still fooling around with Ernie."

"Did you know about the affair between Anna and Ernie before then?" asked Beanie.

Delaney nodded. "Florence had told me. I didn't believe her, but then Anna ..."

"Then, Anna, what?"

"Take a breath and focus," Roger coached.

Inhaling, Delaney trembled as she released a shaky breath. "Anna told Victoria to leave, and so Victoria left. And then Anna started pacing and saying she had to get out of the house, but she didn't want to go back to the egg hunt. She decided that she would take a walk through the Hibiscus grove, to clear her mind. I told her I would go with her. I don't think she wanted my company, but I followed her. While we were in the grove, I asked Anna if what Victoria had said was true. Was she still sleeping with Ernie even though Victoria had told her to stay away from him?"

"And what did she say?"

"She admitted that she was," said Delaney, wringing her hands. "I asked her if she loved him."

"Did she?" Beanie asked, wary of the glazed look in Delaney's gaze. Her rocking became more pronounced, gaining momentum and velocity.

"She laughed at me," said Delaney, voice rising, a hint of indignation in her tone. "She asked me was I serious? I told her I was. She said she wasn't in love with Ernie. She didn't even like the sex. She said Ernie was a selfish lover who didn't know how to please a woman. I asked her why was she having an affair with him if she didn't love him or like the sex? Anna told me she'd slept with Ernie so she could make a video of them together to use against him."

Beanie knew about the botched blackmail attempt. But, had Delaney known, on the day of the egg hunt, that Anna's attempts to force Ernie's hand with a sex tape had failed? He was about to ask her when she continued to speak.

"I told Anna that was wrong and Anna laughed at me again and said I was naïve and didn't understand how the world worked," Delaney said. "She said she'd been trying to save her business, and I just told her that was wrong. So wrong. She kept laughing at me and then she said she was going back to the house. When she turned and started to walk away from me, I grabbed a branch that had fallen … and I hit her."

11

"I didn't hit Anna that hard," Delaney swore, her tone beseeching. "Not hard enough to kill her."

Beanie asked, "How do you know Anna wasn't dead after you hit her?"

"She wasn't dead. I promise you," said Delaney, wringing her shaking hands. "I swear she wasn't dead! She wasn't dead!"

Concerned for Delaney's mental well-being, Beanie glanced at Roger, wondering if the man thought the interview had become detrimental to his wife. Or, was he willing to allow Delaney to continue, even though her eyes were wild and glassy. Beanie hoped the woman wasn't about to have another episode like the one she'd experienced at the egg hunt.

"I allowed my anger to get out of control, and I hit Anna with a tree branch." Delaney twisted the ends of the shawl into a knot, then untied the knot, and then twisted the ends into a knot again. "It was wrong of me, I know, but I didn't take my medicine, and—"

Roger cleared his throat and stood, pulling Delaney to her feet. "Sweetheart, I think you've had enough for today, and you need to rest."

Looking confused, her eyes furtive, Delaney nodded.

"Please excuse me, Roland," said Roger. "I'm just going to take Delaney upstairs, and I'll return shortly."

Beanie nodded, thankful that Roger had decided to cut the interview short. Slumping back against the couch, he exhaled, unsure of what to think about Delaney's bizarre story. He wasn't sure if he believed the disturbed woman. He also didn't know what evidence the police had against her. He'd have to call Officer Fields for an update. Until then, he had to take Delaney at her word—which, admittedly, seemed far-fetched. Her hysterical rambling was hardly credible. However, even more implausible was her insistence that she'd hit Delaney, but hadn't killed her.

Maybe Delaney hadn't killed Anna with a tree branch, but suppose she'd grabbed a knife from the kitchen before she followed Anna outside and into the Hibiscus grove? She might have struck Anna in the head to render her unconscious and then stabbed her to death.

Standing, Beanie walked toward the ceiling-to-floor windows and stared out at the back lawn.

It was entirely possible that everything Delaney had told him was a figment of her imagination. The woman was a perfect candidate for an extended stay at the Rakestraw-Blake Center in the Aerie Islands. On the other hand, the police had arrested her. They wouldn't have locked Delaney up if there wasn't evidence tying her to Anna's murder.

"Sorry about that ..."

Beanie turned and headed toward the center of the room. "No worries. She going to be okay?"

"Not if she doesn't beat these charges against her." His expression grim, Roger strode toward Beanie. "If you're not able to find a better suspect and she's put on trial—"

"Don't get ahead of yourself, okay?" Beanie cautioned. "Don't think the worst unless you absolutely have to."

Scoffing, Roger shook his head as he walked past Beanie, stopping in front of the windows. "I'm starting to think I do have to think the worst.

Delaney made a scene, worse than that one you just witnessed, at the police station."

"What kind of scene?" Beanie asked.

Roger exhaled. "Didn't exactly do herself any favors, screaming and screeching. I thought they might have to use a Taser on her, but I was able to calm her down. Of course, her manic hysteria convinced that bastard Janvier that she's a homicidal maniac."

"Janvier has been wrong before," said Beanie. "He was ready to swear on a stack of Bibles that Noelle was guilty, but that couldn't have been further from the truth."

Roger faced him. "I just don't understand. I was sure the police were going to arrest Ted."

"You think Ted killed Anna?" asked Beanie.

Shoving his hands into his slacks, Roger said, "I don't know. I spoke to Florence, and she'd discovered that the police had found the murder weapon on Ted's property. And then I heard—again from Florence— that Ted had been questioned by the police for several hours. I just assumed his arrest was imminent."

"Did the police come here to arrest Delaney?"

"They asked us to come down to the station to give statements," said Roger. "Initially, I balked because my family and I had left the egg hunt before Anna was murdered. What light could we possibly shed on anything? Janvier insisted. When we arrived, he started badgering Delaney with questions. She became hysterical, and Janvier had her arrested for Anna's murder."

"What evidence does Janvier have on her?"

"He wouldn't explicitly say," Roger said. "Just told me that he had more than enough conclusive evidence to arrest my wife."

Making a mental note to ask Officer Fields about the evidence against Delaney, Beanie asked, "What do you think of Delaney's story?"

Roger's eyes narrowed. "Are you asking me if I think my wife killed Anna?"

"Do you?" challenged Beanie.

With a exhale, Roger rubbed his jaw. "I believe my wife."

Nodding, Beanie said, "Well, I should probably get going."

"I'll walk you out," Roger said.

In the foyer, the cardiologist said, "Roland, I appreciate your willingness to help Delaney. Just as you believed in your wife, I believe in my wife."

"I can't make any promises," warned Beanie.

Grabbing the knob on the left side of the double door, Roger said, "I understand. Your best efforts will be more than enough."

As Beanie crossed the threshold, something Delaney had said came to his mind. Facing Roger, he said, "Before I go, I wanted to ask you …"

Standing in the doorway, Roger waited.

Beanie thought he detected a flash of impatience, but still, he asked, "Delaney didn't take her medication on the day of the egg hunt?"

Roger stared at him, a strange emotion flickering across his stern face. "My wife was confused. She took her meds that day. She takes them every day. I make sure of it."

12

After lunch with Noelle at a park near the marina, a few streets over from the pharmacy she managed, Beanie went back to the Palmchat Gazette to do some fact-checking and make a few phone calls regarding his PC-5 political piece but found his heart wasn't in it.

He still felt like crap for putting his wife in the position of having to choose between helping him advance his career and opening up old wounds. The scars left behind by her father were deeper than Beanie realized. Scars that still hadn't healed. Scars Noelle kept hidden.

Beanie knew the relationship between Noelle and her father was damaged, irrevocably broken, and probably wouldn't be repaired. But, he didn't know why. Why couldn't his wife talk to her father? What was stopping her? Or was the question – who was stopping her?

He glanced at the wedding photo he kept on his desk. He and the most beautiful girl he'd ever seen, immortalized in a moment of pure joy, smiling and happy, eager to start their life as a couple, together forever, no matter what, to the very end, whether it was bitter or sweet.

If Roger really felt the same way about Delaney as Beanie did about Noelle, then he couldn't blame the man for going out of his way, and swallowing his pride, to make sure his wife didn't go down for something she hadn't done.

Beanie rubbed his chin. He still wasn't sure about helping the Pinkertons find a better suspect, but Roger's emotional blackmail had worked. Beanie loathed Detective Janvier. The thought of the man jumping to more erroneous conclusions in his single-minded quest to close a case as quickly as possible pissed him off.

His mind more or less made up, Beanie put his PC-5 notes away, grabbed a fresh notepad, and then scrolled through the contacts in his phone.

Ten minutes later, he'd reached Victoria DuVert, the volatile girl he'd known, and mostly avoided, in high school. After quick pleasantries, Victoria said, "So, you want a quote from me about Anna's murder?"

"I'm trying to talk to most of the guests who were at the egg hunt," said Beanie, deciding to tread lightly. He didn't want to antagonize Victoria if he could help it. She was known to go from zero to bitch in sixty seconds or less.

"Or maybe you want to ask me if I killed Anna?"

"Why would I want to ask you that?"

"Because Ernie told you that I threatened to kill Anna because she slept with him," said Victoria.

"Surprised Ernie told you about our conversation," remarked Beanie.

"Me and my husband don't lie to each other," said Victoria. "The truth hurts sometimes, but the pain of a lie never ends."

Something told Beanie that she meant physical pain, not emotional pain. "Did you kill Anna?"

"My husband thinks I did," admitted Victoria. "But, I didn't. I mean, sure I look suspicious because I told her to stay away from Ernie, but like I told the cops—"

"The police questioned you?"

"Detective Janvier tried to get me to admit that I wanted Anna dead, but that wasn't true," said Victoria. "I just wanted her to leave my husband alone. I thought I had made that clear to her, but I found out they'd hooked up again—at the egg hunt! Can you believe that?"

Beanie's mouth dropped open. "Anna and Ernie had sex at the egg hunt? Where? When? How do you know that? Did you catch them?"

"Belinda caught them in the pantry," said Victoria. "She told me. I was pissed. So, when Anna faked that migraine, and then Delaney and Belinda went to check on her, I went too, but not to see how she was doing. I was going to give that dirty bitch a piece of my mind. I was going to let her know for once and for all that if she didn't stay away from Ernie, I was going to …"

Victoria trailed off.

Beanie listened, waiting. All he heard was a flurry of outdoor noises. Tires on asphalt and car horns, rushing wind and occasional bursts of distant conversation.

"Victoria?" prompted Beanie, wondering if she could still hear him.

"I didn't kill Anna," said Victoria.

"But you argued with her at the egg hunt," said Beanie, remembering Delany's version of events. "Anna was on the computer, and—"

"The bitch was ignoring me," said Victoria. "And I will not be ignored. I wanted her to hear what I had to say, so I yanked her ass up and told her."

"And then what?"

"And then I left," said Victoria. "I wasn't even at the house when Anna was killed, which I told the cops."

"Who do you think killed Anna?" Beanie asked.

"I haven't really thought much about who did it," said Victoria.

"You think Delaney killed her?" asked Beanie.

Scoffing, Victoria said, "Delaney is bonkers, okay? I would never dispute that. But, would she commit murder? Depends …"

"On what?"

"You might have noticed that Delaney doesn't seem to have a mind of her own," said Victoria. "All of her decisions are made for her."

"What do you mean?" asked Beanie, not sure he understood the meaning behind Victoria's insinuation.

"If Delaney killed Anna," said Victoria, "then Roger told her to do it."

13

"Delaney is absolutely capable of murder," announced Florence Taylor.

Rubbing his jaw, Beanie stared across the table at the Taylors, who were dressed alike in jaunty pastel orange colors and greedily partook in coffee and the leftover donuts from the *Palmchat Gazette* staff meeting in the conference room this morning.

Beanie had been ruminating over his conversation with Victoria when the receptionist, Millie, buzzed him to announce that he had visitors. Chuck and Florence Taylor had stopped by the offices to provide him with interesting tidbits for his follow-up story, which they thought should have a little more pizazz, and a bit more zing, than the initial piece: MURDER AT AVALON ESTATES EGG HUNT.

At first, Beanie had wondered if he should be offended, but he knew the gossipy couple was right. The follow-up couldn't be phoned in, written as an afterthought. The piece would need a stronger hook, Beanie knew. And a more interesting angle. Some context and subtext wouldn't hurt, either. After he heard from Officer Fields, who he hoped would give him information on the evidence against Delaney, Beanie would write the story. Not that he had a choice in the matter. During the staff meeting, Vivian had given him a not-so-subtle reminder that she wanted the follow-up in her inbox this afternoon.

"Why do you think Delaney is capable of murder?" asked Beanie, not inclined to believe anything the Taylors had to say, and yet he had to be objective, unbiased.

"Delaney has been off-and-on different kinds of meds for the past few months," said Florence.

"Some days, she's lucid," said Chuck. "Other days she's looney."

"You think she could have killed Anna during one of her looney moments?" asked Beanie, recalling Roger's insistence that Delaney had taken her meds on the day of the egg hunt, despite his wife's confession that she hadn't. The Taylors' gossip seemed to corroborate Roger's claim that Delaney had been confused about not taking her meds.

"That's when Delaney attacks," said Florence. "When she's off her meds, or the doctors are trying to regulate her medication. That's when she has the potential to become homicidal."

"Delaney was in between medications the last time she attacked Anna," said Chuck, then shoved a jelly donut in his mouth.

"The last time she attacked Anna?" Beanie stared at Chuck, though the man's open-mouth chewing made him slightly queasy.

"About two months ago," said Florence. "As I understand it—because I wasn't there, but I have a friend who was and told me all about it—Anna and Belinda were having a tense conversation at the boutique. Delaney was there to have lunch with Belinda and overheard the argument, which took place in the stockroom."

Wiping a dollop of jelly from the side of his mouth, Chuck said, "Apparently, Anna and Belinda got into it about declining sales at the boutique. Each of them blamed the other."

"Belinda designs all the clothes for the boutique," said Florence, taking a sip of coffee. "Their selling point is that all items are island originals. Well, Anna said that Belinda's designs weren't appealing to their customer base, which is the upscale, chic, wealthy traveler who expects island luxury."

"Naturally, Belinda, being a creative type, was hurt by Anna's stinging rebuke of her designs," said Chuck. "She burst into tears and fled the boutique."

"You didn't hear this from me," said Florence, an octave above sotto voce, "but Belinda's designs aren't very good anymore. Belinda used to know exactly what their customers wanted, but now she's into mixing styles and lots of experimenting."

"Anyway, Delaney screamed at Anna for being cruel to Belinda," said Chuck. "She grabbed a pair of scissors and lunged at Anna, who ran screaming out onto the sales floor. Delaney ran after her, and another customer had to restrain Delaney."

"You're kidding," remarked Beanie, wondering why Roger hadn't mentioned Delaney's previous attack on Anna. Had the cardiologist thought Beanie wouldn't help Delaney if he knew about her previous aggressions against the victim?

"Anna pressed charges, but then she dropped them," said Florence. "Apparently, Roger convinced Anna that Delaney's new meds had made her volatile."

Reaching for the last donut, Chuck said, "As long as Delaney takes her medicine then she's okay and not at risk to hurt someone."

"What kind of medicine does she take?" asked Beanie, tapping a pen against the notepad in front of him.

"Anti-psychotics," answered Florence.

"She's schizophrenic," supplied Chuck.

"She hears voices," said Florence.

"They tell her to hurt people," said Chuck.

Disturbed by the Taylors' revelations, Beanie asked, "Who do you think killed Anna?"

"It's got to be Ted," said Chuck

"Or Ernie," said Florence

"Why Ted? Asked Beanie

Chuck shrugged. "Isn't it always the husband?"

Beanie looked at Florence. "Why Ernie?"

"Because if it's not the husband, then it's usually the secret lover."

14

"Normally, I don't agree with Janvier's theories because let's face it, he's usually wrong," said Officer Damon Fields, who'd finally returned Beanie's call.

For the past three hours, Beanie had been trying to reach the officer, who had proven time and again to be an invaluable source for the *Palmchat Gazette*.

"He rushes to judgment, and he's got a raging case of confirmation bias."

"Confirmation bias," said Beanie. "That's when you come to a premature conclusion and then look for evidence that will confirm your conclusion, whether the evidence makes sense, or not."

"Another problem with Janvier is that he doesn't concern himself with the motive," groused Fields. "He focuses on the 'means' and the 'opportunity.' If he can put the suspect at the location of the crime and connect the suspect to the murder weapon, then that's enough for him."

"Doesn't matter if the suspect had no reason to kill the victim," said Beanie.

"Exactly," said Fields. "Anyway, as I said, I usually don't trust Janvier's theories, but this time, I think he might be right about Delaney Pinkerton."

"Why's that?" asked Beanie, reaching for a pen and a notepad, anxious to find out why Detective Janvier believed Delaney Pinkerton had killed Anna Zamora.

"The evidence does point to Delaney Pinkerton as the killer," said Fields. "And it's not just circumstantial. The evidence is backed up by science."

"What evidence did Janvier find?" asked Beanie, worried that the evidence might be strong enough to impede his efforts to find a better suspect for Anna's murder. If the evidence against Delaney was solid, there might not be a better suspect.

"Janvier was convinced that Ted Zamora had killed his wife," began Fields, "until the CSI guys told him about a piece of torn fabric found in Anna's hand."

"Torn fabric?" echoed Beanie, remembering the moment when Delaney Pinkerton had stumbled out of the lemon orchard. Had her shirt been torn?

"A patch of lavender-colored silk," said Fields. "Looked like it came from a woman's blouse or maybe a tie. Anyway, Janvier inquired about what the guests at the egg hunt had been wearing. This couple came forth—"

"Chuck and Florence Taylor?"

"How'd you know?" asked Fields.

Beanie groaned. "Apparently, they know everything there is to know about everyone in Avalon Estates."

"That's what they told Janvier," said Fields. "He got a lot of information from them."

"And I'm sure he didn't have to twist their arms," quipped Beanie.

"They were more than happy to give their statements," said Fields. "They told Janvier about Mrs. Pinkerton's strange episode at the egg hunt. And then they went on to detail a time two months ago when Delaney Pinkerton attacked Anna Zamora. Then the Taylors told Janvier that Delaney Pinkerton had worn a silk lavender top to the egg hunt—which Delaney Pinkerton admitted."

"She didn't do herself any favors," said Beanie, wondering why Roger Pinkerton had allowed his wife to be questioned without an attorney, considering the woman's fragile mental state.

"Janvier sent a team over to collect the lavender shirt when Delaney was in jail," said Fields. "The CSI guys found the shirt. The fabric fibers contained dirt from the Hibiscus grove at the Zamora estate. So, Janvier was able to put Delaney Pinkerton at the crime scene."

"What's the science-backed evidence?" asked Beanie.

"We found the branch that was used to hit Anna Zamora in the head," said Fields. "The bark contained traces of the victim's blood and skin, which we suspected. But, there was also blood that didn't belong to the victim. That blood was a match for Delaney Pinkerton, whose DNA was taken when she was arrested for attacking Anna Zamora a few months ago. Those charges were dropped, but our policy is to destroy DNA after six months, so we still had Mrs. Pinkerton's DNA on file."

"Okay, so Delaney admitted that she hit Anna in the head," said Beanie. "But, Anna didn't die from the head wound, right? She died as a result of the stab wounds, I'm assuming."

"You're right," confirmed Fields. "The blade severed Anna Zamora's heart."

"What does Janvier have to tie Delaney Pinkerton to the murder weapon? Are her fingerprints on the knife?"

"There were no fingerprints on the knife," said Fields. "Anna's blood was on the blade, obviously. But, we found a pair of discarded thin polyethylene gloves, the kind cafeteria worker's use for food prep, in the trash at the Zamora house. The gloves had traces of Anna's blood, and there was substantial sweat DNA inside the gloves."

Sweat DNA in gloves wrote Beanie on his notepad. He was familiar with the somewhat controversial theory—the belief that a person's sweat contained enough DNA to identify that person. While investigating the murder of an engineer who'd been decapitated, sweat DNA had been recovered and used to catch the killer.

"Was it Delaney Pinkerton's sweat?" asked Beanie, knowing that the woman didn't stand a chance if her DNA was found on gloves covered in Anna Zamora's blood.

"Not sure yet," said Fields. "Janvier just sent the gloves to the Rakestraw-Blake Center. They got that state-of-the-art forensic lab on their campus. It was created for the Aerie Islands cops, but the RBC doesn't mind helping us out. Anyway, Janvier hopes to get the results by the end of the week, and he's certain the sweat DNA will be a match for Delaney Pinkerton."

Exhaling, Beanie said, "I can see how you might be inclined to agree with Janvier, but Delaney might not have been in her right mind when she confessed," said Beanie, wondering if Octavia Constant would say her client had been coerced into incriminating herself during a moment when she was mentally incapacitated.

"I hate to say that I think Janvier got it right this time," said Fields.

"If any other detective besides Janvier was working this case," said Beanie, "I would absolutely believe Delaney Pinkerton was guilty, but ..."

"But, after what Janvier did to Noelle," said Fields, "I know you'll always question his judgment. I don't blame you."

Beanie thanked Fields for talking to him and was about to end the call when the officer stopped him.

"Before you go," said Fields. "I wanted to ask you: does Noelle have a sister?"

Thrown by the question, Beanie said, "Not that I know of ..."

"What do you mean? Not that you know of?" Fields laughed. "She's your wife, man. You should know if she's got a sister, or not. You know your wife, right?"

"Yeah, right, what I meant was ..." Beanie trailed off, trying to collect his thoughts. "No, Noelle doesn't have a sister. Why do you ask?"

As Fields lamented about his mother, who was hoping he would get married soon, Beanie chuckled and tried to commiserate, but he wasn't really listening, only slightly paying attention.

The officer's question had sobered him. You know your wife, right? Beanie did know his wife, and yet sometimes, he didn't. Sometimes, he felt he only knew what Noelle wanted him to know. He wondered if the things she'd shared with him about her past were entirely true. Or, was she still keeping things from him? And did he even want to know everything about his wife?

Or was he content with knowing just the things about her which confirmed that she was the woman he wanted to spend the rest of his life with?

15

"The PC-5 killed Anna," said Bob Davenport, stopping in front of a wall of bookshelves, where he bent over, picked up a doll, and tossed it into a large square rattan basket.

Beanie stared at the dedicated stay-at-home dad and house husband of Belinda, who'd co-owned the boutique with Anna. Beanie wished Bob would forget the housework and focus on what he wanted to tell him. Bob's phone call, two hours ago, had been vague. Bob wanted to see him and had something very important to tell him, but he couldn't talk about it over the phone. Beanie had agreed to meet him during lunch.

When Beanie arrived at the Davenport home, Bob had opened the door apologizing for the mess in the family room, which featured West Indian and British Colonial furniture with mirrored accent pieces, lots of bold, chintz fabric and glitzy accessories. His girls were at a private ballet lesson, which gave him time to tidy up the living area.

"The PC-5?" echoed Beanie.

Near a wall of sliding pocket doors that looked out to the side yard, Bob picked up coloring books and added them to the collection of toys he'd tossed into the basket.

"I read your story in the *Palmchat Gazette* this morning," said Bob, dropping a stuffed animal into the rattan basket and then faced Beanie. "You didn't get the facts right. Delaney Pinkerton didn't have anything to do with Anna's death. The PC-5 killed her. Your readers need to know that."

Exhaling, Beanie rubbed his jaw. He'd finished his follow-up late yesterday evening, and after a few edits from Vivian, the piece had been published on the paper's website and in the early morning print edition. SUSPECT ARRESTED IN EGG HUNT MURDER was doing well, getting lots of clicks and page reads. Most of the online comments suggested that the public believed Delaney was the killer.

But now Bob was blaming Anna's murder on the island cartel?

"Why do you think the gang killed her?" asked Beanie.

Walking toward the couch where Beanie sat, Bob stopped to pick up more dolls and toss them into the basket. "The PC-5 wanted protection money from Anna. Meaning, if she wanted to keep doing business, she would have to pay them not to target her business and to "protect" the business from theft, vandalism."

Beanie knew how the PC-5 protection tax worked. Good, hard-working people trying to feed their families were forced to allow the PC-5 to protect their businesses. Lots of business owners were unable to pay the tax, which was a cruel form of usury, and were then forced to take loans from the PC-5 to pay the tax. Inevitably, they were unable to pay off their loans, and then the PC-5 would force the owners to sell their business to the cartel. More often than not, the business was used as a legitimate entity through which PC-5 funds were laundered. The sick cycle of forced financial ruin was unofficially known as a tenant of Brazonomics, named after the Brazos family, which controlled the cartel's financial division.

Bob said, "Anna refused to pay the tax and then all of a sudden, declining sales. Anna tried to blame it on Belinda's new designs, but it was the PC-5."

"You tell the cops that?" Beanie asked.

Placing the rattan basket on the coffee table, Bob shook his head.

"Belinda told me to keep my mouth shut because I have no proof and snitching on the PC-5 is dangerous. Me, her, and the kids could all end up on the Death List."

Beanie rubbed his jaw. "What about proof?"

Bob exhaled. "That's why Belinda wanted me to stay quiet. I don't have any proof."

"How did you find out that the PC-5 approached Anna about paying the protection tax?"

"Anna told Belinda," said Bob. "Belinda told me. My wife was very upset because Anna blamed her. Belinda said Anna thought their boutique was targeted for the protection tax because of ... my wife's past ..."

"Her past?" Beanie repeated, a sly uneasiness settling within him.

Bob frowned. "I'm sure Chuck and Florence were only too happy to tell you that Belinda was once in the PC-5."

"They mentioned it," admitted Beanie, his uneasiness segueing into anxiousness.

"I'm not surprised," said Bob, dropping down on the couch across from Beanie. "Belinda has worked damn hard to put that life behind her. She's not that person anymore, but Chuck and Florence pretend not to know, or maybe they don't believe that my wife has changed."

"Some people don't want you to forget the past," said Beanie.

"Does Noelle have that problem?" Bob asked.

Beanie's stomach twisted. "What problem?"

"People constantly reminding her that she used to be in the gang," said Bob. "People unwilling to believe that she turned her life around?"

Uncomfortable and annoyed with the direction of the conversation, Beanie said, "Not really."

Nodding, Bob said, "Can I ask you something?"

Beanie hesitated. He wasn't in the mood for questions about Noelle and her connection to the PC-5. Just thinking about his wife's past with the cartel was enough to trigger feelings of disappointment and confusion.

"Okay, sure," said Beanie, already regretting his decision.

"Did you always know about Noelle?" asked Bob. "That she was in the PC-5, I mean?"

Scratching his eyebrow, Beanie said, "No, I didn't."

Bob nodded. "Same here. I found out a few years ago. It was a shock. Almost tore our marriage apart. I was angry that she didn't tell me."

Beanie nodded. He knew the feeling and could commiserate.

"More than that," Bob went on, "I was livid that she'd allowed the cartel to fool her into thinking that the PC-5 was her only choice. I couldn't understand why she'd joined the gang. I'd grown up hating the PC-5. I vowed to never have anything to do with them."

"I hear you," said Beanie. He'd always despised the cartel. Growing up, hearing stories of the cartel's brutal savagery, Beanie had decided he would never join the gang.

Bob said, "But, Belinda grew up in the foster system. No guidance or direction. No affection or encouragement. It was probably inevitable, unavoidable that she would gravitate toward the cartel because they made her feel safe and accepted. That's why those low-life island thugs are so damn dangerous. They prey upon the weak and the impressionable and the abandoned and rejected. But Belinda got free from them."

"How?" asked Beanie.

"How?" Bob blinked, confusion crossing his features.

Beanie said, "Usually, it's blood in, blood out."

"We didn't really talk about how Belinda got out," said Bob. "That didn't matter. What mattered was that she got away from those monsters and got her life back on track."

16

"Looks like I'm going to be writing about the PC-5 after all," said Beanie, leaning on the pillows arranged against the headboard.

After baths and bedtime stories, the boys were in bed. Beanie looked forward to spending time with his wife, who had become more interested in jumping *his* bones since he'd apologized for asking her to facilitate a meeting between him and her father.

"What do you mean?" asked Noelle, crawling across the bed toward him. "Thought you were putting the cartel political story on hold?"

Beanie pulled her closer to him, into the crook of his arm, and kissed her forehead. "I met with Bob Davenport today. He claims the PC-5 killed Anna Zamora."

"What?" Noelle moved her head to look at him. "That's crazy."

After giving his wife the details about the conversation with Bob, Beanie said, "Of course, he has no proof."

"He might be telling the truth, though," said Noelle.

"You think?"

"I never had anything to do with the protection tax," said Noelle. "Taxes are about money, and anything that has to do with money is run by Brazos."

"The financial arm of the cartel," said Beanie, stroking his wife's arm as he wondered where the conversation would lead.

"But I knew about the protection tax because ..."

"Because?" Beanie prompted, though he wasn't sure he wanted to know how Noelle knew about the gang's protection racket.

His wife curled closer to him and said, "Because if you refuse to pay the protection tax, then someone from Vadaj would be sent to make you change your mind."

Vadaj, Beanie knew, was the enforcement and security division of the cartel, solely responsible for causing physical harm, inflicting pain, and taking lives, including those on the dreaded Death List.

"My father started out as a convincer for Vadaj," said Noelle. "His job was to convince you to pay the protection tax, which he did. Dad was very good at convincing people."

Beanie stared at the palmetto-leaf ceiling fan swirling lazily overhead, thinking about the word, 'convincing.' An interesting euphemism for a beat down murder, he thought.

Noelle sighed. "Anyway, from what I know about protection, low-level guys—the street crew worker bees—will use it as a power move when they're trying to move up in the cartel. They try to prove their worth by bringing in income. They come up with a scam and put it in play. If the scam is successful in generating lots of money, the bee might be sanctioned to continue the scam."

"And then what would happen?" asked Beanie.

"If the scam continued to make money for the gang without any issues with law enforcement, then the low-level guy would be sanctioned to manage a small crew, and if his crew was successful with the scam, then the bee could be promoted to a supervisor."

"What happens if he's promoted?" asked Beanie, amazed at how the cartel functioned like a corporate entity.

"The bee could work his way up to a manager, and then, to a Director, which is the highest title or rank a non-family member can achieve, and it's a serious position," said Noelle. "There are only a handful of Directors in each family, no more than three, but they direct all activities of the managers, supervisors, and street crews."

"Fascinating," said Beanie, thinking of how he might incorporate the information into his PC-5 political piece.

"Can't believe I just told you that," said Noelle, throwing her forearm over her eyes as she groaned.

"Can't believe I haven't picked your brain about the PC-5 before," said Beanie. "The source I've been looking for has been lying next to me all this time."

Removing her arm, Noelle stared at him. "Are you serious, Roland?"

Beanie tried to temper his disappointment as his wife moved away from him. He hadn't meant to upset Noelle again by bringing up the same issues they'd fought about. Issues they'd gotten past and moved on from. "Babe, I'm sorry, I didn't mean to—"

"No, it's okay." Noelle sat up and tucked her legs beneath her. "Don't apologize. I'm the one who's sorry."

Worried, Beanie sat forward. "About what?"

"I should have told you that I was in the gang," said Noelle.

"Well, it's not like I asked," said Beanie, hoping to lighten the mood.

Noelle shook her head and sighed. "I didn't want to tell you because I never wanted you to know. I kept it from you because I knew how you felt about the PC-5. I didn't want you to feel that way about me. I didn't want to be dishonest, but I didn't want to lose you."

Beanie reached across the short distance between them and took his wife's hands. "Do I wish you had told me? Yes. But, it bothers me that you thought I would leave you because you used to be in the PC-5. Even if I wanted to, I could never leave you."

"If you had known I'd been in the cartel when you first met me," said Noelle, "would you have asked me out?"

Beanie frowned. "I can't believe you asked me that."

Noelle exhaled. "Will you just answer me?"

Shaking his head, Beanie said, "Yes, I would have. Absolutely. Definitely."

"Liar," said Noelle, adding a sly smile.

Thankful that his wife's mood was improving, Beanie pulled her into his arms and was about to kiss her when his cell phone beeped.

Beanie cursed. "Who the hell is texting me at eleven o'clock at night?"

Noelle grabbed the phone from the nightstand, unlocked it, and stared at the screen. "Octavia Constant."

Groaning, Beanie took the phone from Noelle. "She probably wants an update on my progress in the search for a better suspect in Anna Zamora's murder."

"Or maybe she's upset about the article you wrote," said Noelle.

"Why would she be upset?"

"Maybe because you made her client look like a murderer?" Noelle shrugged.

"Maybe her client is a murderer," said Beanie. "I didn't try to make Delaney Pinkerton look guilty. Yes, I mentioned that she'd attacked Anna before, but I also said the charges were dropped. That was balanced reporting."

"But you didn't offer a better suspect," said Noelle.

"I don't think there is a better suspect," said Beanie. "I think I should tell Octavia, and Roger, that I can't help them."

"That's probably a good idea," agreed his wife as she took the phone from him, put it back on the nightstand and then stretched out on top of him. "But call her in the morning and tell her. Right now, you have better things to do."

17

"Anna was lying about the PC-5 targeting the boutique for the protection tax," said Belinda, carrying several colorful dresses as she strutted around a display of flower-printed sarongs and scarfs with matching accessories.

Circling the four-tiered gondola shelf, made of mahogany and flanked by tall, fake palm trees, the glamorous designer stopped to add the dresses to a short rack that extended from the shelf.

Beanie had decided to stop by the boutique before heading into the *Palmchat Gazette*, around eight in the morning. The boutique didn't open for another two hours, but Beanie took a chance that Belinda would arrive early to prepare for the day.

"Why would Anna lie about the protection tax?" asked Beanie.

"She was trying to hide her financial ineptness," said Belinda, arranging the accessories on the shelves. "When Anna and I opened the boutique, I was so excited. I'd be able to showcase my designing talent without having to worry about the books and the finances and the day to day operations. Anna assured me that she could handle the business side of the boutique."

"How did you find out that Anna wasn't as business savvy as she claimed to be?" Beanie asked.

Stepping back to survey her work, Belinda shook her head and began rearranging scarves and necklaces. "I found out we were in arrears with most of our vendors and very close to being evicted. Then I had a conversation with our banker who told me that Anna had been withdrawing large sums of money each week. When I confronted Anna, she claimed she was paying the PC-5 protection money."

Stroking his jaw, Beanie asked, "How do you know she wasn't?"

Belinda circled the display again, pausing next to the rack where she'd placed the dresses. "This isn't going to work."

"What?" asked Beanie.

"This display," said Belinda, tapping her bottom lip with her forefinger. "I need it to invoke a specific mood."

"A specific mood?" Beanie repeated, glancing at the designer.

"Colonial chic," said Belinda. "Something's missing."

"Or, maybe something doesn't belong," suggested Beanie as he stared at the display, which looked fine to him, but he wasn't really sure what colonial chic was.

Belinda gave him a shrewd glance. "I asked some old PC-5 contacts if Anna was paying the protection tax and they said our business isn't on the protection list."

"You're still in contact with the PC-5?" asked Beanie.

"Well, unlike some former cartel members," said Belinda, crossing her arms. "I don't turn my back on the people who were there for me when I needed them the most just because I made it out of the hood and made a new life for myself."

Beanie recognized the designer's not-so-subtle dig at Noelle, but he chose not to be distracted by anger or indignation.

"My husband shouldn't have told you that the PC-5 killed Anna," said Belinda. "And I hope you won't put that in your next article. You could cause a lot of problems for my family if you did."

"What kind of problems?" Beanie asked.

Belinda exhaled. "Ask your wife. She'll tell you that accusing the gang of a crime they didn't commit is a quick way to get on the Death List."

Struggling to control his anger, Beanie said, "If Bob is right and Anna was on the Death List—"

"The PC-5 didn't have anything to do with Anna's murder," said Belinda. "And Delaney Pinkerton didn't kill her, either."

"So, if it wasn't the PC-5, and it wasn't Delaney," said Beanie, "then who killed Anna?"

Belinda's glance turned into a glare. "Her husband killed her."

"Why would Ted kill his wife?"

"Anna had something on him," said Belinda, snatching a scarf from the shelf and draping it around one of the dresses hanging on the rack. "She tried to blackmail him."

Doubtful of Belinda's claims, Beanie asked, "Anna tried to extort money from her own husband?"

"It didn't work," said Belinda. "He's basically broke. A millionaire on paper."

"What did she have on him?"

Shrugging, Belinda said, "I have no idea. But, she was trying to get reward money from the Palmchat Islands Investigative Bureau for turning him in."

"Why was Anna withdrawing money from the boutique's bank account?" asked Beanie. "You said it wasn't to pay the PC-5."

"I told you Ted was broke," said Belinda. "They needed money to fund their lifestyle. They lived well above their means."

"So, wait a minute," said Beanie, his suspicions growing. "You're saying that Anna was stealing money from the boutique and trying to blackmail Ted and hoping to get a monetary reward for snitching on her husband just to live in Avalon Estates?"

"You don't have money, so I don't expect you to understand," said Belinda, sneering at him. "But, when you're rich, you'll do anything to stay rich, even if that means you have to kill someone."

18

"I don't trust Roger Pinkerton," said Octavia Constant, finishing the last of her grilled goat salad.

Sitting across from the attorney at a table in the park of Pourciau Square, Beanie gnawed on the two or three fries left from the goat burger meal he'd inhaled. Following his testy exchange with Belinda Davenport, Beanie had headed to the *Palmchat Gazette* office where he'd returned Octavia's text, agreeing to meet her for lunch.

It was a nice day for dining al fresco, beautiful and sunny, the kind of weather tourists paid thousands of dollars to experience. The square was busy, crowded with locals and visitors taking advantage of the lovely surroundings.

"Why not?" asked Beanie, though he shared Octavia's feelings toward the cardiologist. Something about Roger Pinkerton was … sinister.

"He didn't tell me that his wife attacked Anna Zamora three months ago," said Octavia. "I had to read about that in your article."

"I didn't write that Delaney attacked Anna," said Beanie. "I wrote, the suspect, according to police reports, had a previous altercation involving the victim but the charges were dropped."

"Well, I wanted to know more about that previous altercation," said

Octavia, "so I requested the police report, which said that Delaney attacked Anna with a pair of scissors. But, that wasn't even the worst of it."

"What was worse than attacking Anna with scissors?" asked Beanie.

Stabbing a plastic fork into a strip of goat meat, Octavia said, "The detective assigned to the scissor attack did some digging into Delaney's past. She has a pattern of homicidal rage, something else Roger Pinkerton didn't tell me."

Beanie nodded. "I'd heard she attacked a cafeteria worker when she was in high school."

Octavia said, "She's done much more than that."

"Like what?"

"Last year, Delaney was arrested for trying to run a man off the road," said Octavia. "A colleague of Roger Pinkerton's, a fellow doctor Roger had issues with. She stalked the colleague, began sending threatening notes to the man and following him."

Beanie was shocked. "Are you serious?"

"Delaney was caught when she tried to run the colleague off the road, but he outmaneuvered her and got away—with the license plate of her car. When Delaney was questioned, she claimed that Roger said the man needed to be scared off."

"Did Roger tell Delaney to scare the man?" Beanie asked.

Octavia said, "The cop asked Delaney that question, but she claimed she couldn't remember. All she could remember was that Roger said the man needed to be scared, and then the man would stop bothering him."

"Did the cops question Roger?"

Lips pursed, Octavia rolled her eyes. "Roger Pinkerton told the cops that Delaney was off her meds, which he had encouraged because the particular meds she was on at the time turned her into a zombie and she scared the kids."

Flabbergasted, Beanie shook his head. "I can't believe this."

"I can," said Octavia. "It's entirely possible that Roger Pinkerton took advantage of his wife's mental illness by coercing her to kill Anna Zamora."

"Is there proof of that?"

Octavia shook her head. "I wish there was because that's how I could get Delaney off. She wasn't in control of her mental faculties. She was used as a weapon. There are cases of that, but I'm not sure this is one of them. As I said, I don't trust Roger Pinkerton, but I'm wondering, why would he want Anna Zamora dead?"

Beanie nodded. "What possible motive could he have?"

"That's what I'd like you to help me find out," said Octavia.

"What about the better suspect?" Beanie asked.

"There is no better suspect," said Octavia. "I think Delaney Pinkerton killed Anna Zamora. If I'm going to get her off, I have to prove that Roger forced his wife to commit cold-blooded murder."

19

"I didn't manipulate my wife," insisted Roger Pinkerton. "The police report was wrong. That cop took Delaney's words out of context."

Phone pressed against his ear, Beanie leaned back in the chair behind his desk. Following lunch with Octavia Constant, and still reeling from the revelations about Delaney's past psychotic behavior, Beanie had returned to the *Palmchat Gazette*. Feeling as though Roger Pinkerton had tried to play him for a fool, Beanie contacted the cardiologist to confront him about his lies of omission.

Scoffing, Beanie asked, "What context did the cop take her words out of?"

The cardiologist sighed. "I did tell Delaney about the problems with my colleague. And I did mention, offhand, that I wished he would leave the hospital, but I didn't think he would. Something would have to scare him off or scare him away. I don't remember my exact words, but I didn't think my wife would take them to heart."

"But you knew Delaney was off her meds," said Beanie. "You also knew that when she was off her meds, she was most likely to carry out acts of psychotic rage."

"I did not direct or force or suggest to Delaney that she should scare the man off," said Roger. "I was devastated and horrified when I found out what she'd done."

"You should have been straight with me about the severity of your wife's issues," said Beanie.

"I know that, and I'm sorry," said Roger. "But, I was desperate, and I thought you wouldn't agree to help Delaney if you knew that, in the past, she had exhibited psychotic behavior when she didn't take her medication."

Beanie exhaled. Would he have refused to help Delaney Pinkerton if he'd known the full extent of her problems? Maybe. Maybe not. He wasn't sure. It was hard to know what he would have done if he'd known better.

"I know what you're thinking," said Roger.

"You do?"

"Delaney told you that she didn't take her meds on the day of the egg hunt," said Roger. "So, now you're wondering if she could have killed Anna for that reason, but I'm telling you that she didn't. Delaney did not kill Anna. There is a better suspect."

"Or maybe there isn't," said Beanie, growing weary of the conversation.

"Octavia Constant said that the only way Delaney will get off is if we find a better suspect," said Roger. "Please tell me that you're still willing to help my wife."

"Octavia has changed her strategy," said Beanie.

"What are you talking about?"

"Give her a call," said Beanie. "I have to go."

Ending the call, Beanie shook his head. He wasn't sure what to do about the Pinkertons. On the one hand, it was entirely possible that Roger was some kind of Svengali, using his wife's mental illness to get rid of his enemies. But on the other hand, he didn't think Roger viewed Anna as an enemy. Unless he was missing something...

Rubbing his jaw, Beanie grabbed his cell phone, scrolled through his contacts, and dialed Ted Zamora. The university president had taken an extended leave of absence after Anna was killed, so Beanie knew he would be home.

Ted answered, and after obligatory pleasantries, Beanie got to the reason for his call.

"Did Roger Pinkerton and Anna have any issues?"

"Issues?" echoed Ted.

"What was their relationship like?" Beanie asked. "Was there any conflict between them, or—"

"Anna did think Roger was too controlling," said Ted. "But, she never confronted the man. Why do you ask?"

"Just wondering," said Beanie, not surprised the call had been a bust. "Sorry to have bothered you."

"It was no bother," said Ted. "In fact, I'm glad you called. Do you have some free time to meet with me this afternoon?"

Beanie quickly checked his schedule, then said, "I'm available. Why do you want to meet?"

"I'd like to speak with you about something very important," said Ted. "And it's not something I can discuss over the phone."

20

"Thank you for agreeing to meet with me," said Ted, taking a sip from the tumbler of scotch he held. Beanie had turned down a glass of the libation when Ted offered him a drink, preferring instead to get to the reason for his presence at the Zamora home.

Beanie wasn't sure why Ted wanted to confide in him. They weren't exactly friends. Sure, the guy was Noelle's boss, but their previous interactions had been few and far between. On the rare occasions that they'd spoken to each other, the conversations had been cordial, but superficial. Beanie couldn't understand why Ted would want to share secrets with a *Palmchat Gazette* reporter. Beanie wasn't conducting an official interview, but anything Ted told him would be considered on the table – unless the university president requested an off the record deal.

Sitting on one of the couches in the spacious living room, Beanie asked, "What do you want to talk to me about? And why couldn't you tell me over the phone?"

Ted exhaled as he took a seat on the couch across from Beanie. Unlike the last time they'd spoken, Ted wasn't disoriented or disheveled. Dressed in trousers and a polo shirt, which Beanie suspected was some sort of cashmere-blend, the grieving widower appeared confident and commanding, in total control of his emotions.

"A week before she died," began Ted, "my wife received several phone calls from a strange man. The man's identity was unknown to me until yesterday when I learned that he is a Palmchat Islands Investigative Bureau agent."

Beanie stroked his jaw. Belinda Davenport had said that Anna was hoping to get a reward for turning Ted in to the PIIBs. At the time, Beanie had thought Belinda was coming up with crazy theories for reasons he didn't understand, but maybe the designer had been telling the truth.

"Why was Anna talking to the PIIBs?" Beanie asked.

Ted said, "I don't know, but I have suspicions."

"Which are?"

"I believe my wife was going to turn me in to the federal police," said Ted.

"Why?" asked Beanie. "Did you do something—"

"Four years ago, at the company I used to work for, Vaughn Pharma, I was accused by the PIIB of implementing a scheme to compensate doctors for prescribing the company's drugs."

"Did you bribe doctors?" Asked Beanie.

Ted took another sip of scotch and stared at Beanie. "What I did was make the company a lot of money. My tactics may have been disagreeable to some. However, I don't think I broke any laws."

"That you know of?" asked Beanie.

Ted cleared his throat. "I did make one crucial mistake—I panicked."

"You panicked?" asked Beanie, confused.

"I asked my executive assistant to destroy documents and digital files, which might appear suspicious," said Ted. "In exchange for her help, my executive assistant requested that I marry her. The way she put it, if she was my wife, she wouldn't be compelled to testify against me. It was the best course of action considering that the PIIB had targeted her, hoping to make her flip on me."

"You married your executive assistant?" asked Beanie. "So, this was before you married Anna?"

Shaking his head, Ted said, "Anna was my executive assistant."

Beanie nodded. "So, your marriage to Anna—"

"Was for convenience, on both of our parts," confirmed Ted. "It was convenient for Anna because she wanted a wealthy husband who could support the lavish lifestyle she coveted. And it was convenient for me because as my wife, she couldn't be forced to rat on me."

"The two of you entered a loveless marriage," said Beanie.

Ted shrugged. "We didn't need love. And it wasn't a tortuous union, I don't want you to think that. We liked each other and had previously had an ongoing sexual relationship, though it was casual. Nothing serious."

Co-workers with benefits, thought Beanie, but he said, "The relationship became serious when you asked Anna to help you destroy documents that might have led to your arrest."

Ted exhaled. "I'd like to know what the PIIB agent and my wife spoke about."

"You want to know if Anna was arranging to turn you over to the island feds?"

"Do you have contacts at the PIIB?" asked Ted, leaning forward to place his empty tumbler on the coffee table.

Beanie stared at the university president. "I know a few people."

"Could you make some inquiries with your contacts?" asked Ted, a slight desperation on his tone. "Could you find out if Anna was going to turn me in?"

"Did Anna have evidence against you?"

"I'm not concerned about any evidence against me because there is none," said Ted. "But, if Anna was going to tell the PIIB that I asked her to destroy documents, then I could face charges for obstructing justice in a federal investigation. What I would need you to find out is—"

"I'll ask around," Beanie said, standing, eager to leave. "But I can't make any promises."

"I appreciate your help," said Ted. He stood and stared at Beanie. "But I would like the promise of your discretion. Do you mind keeping our conversation, and your investigation into Anna's dealings with the PIIBs, out of the *Palmchat Gazette*?"

21

"You lied to Ted Zamora?" asked Noelle.

"Not exactly," said Beanie, enjoying the view of his wife as she walked to the bed.

"You told him you have contacts at the PIIB and you don't," said Noelle. "That's *not exactly* the truth."

"I don't have any direct contacts myself, but Vivian and Leo have contacts they could put me in touch with, and anyway, I was hoping he'd spill more tea if he thought I had access to information he needed," said Beanie. "And I was right. Ted thinks Anna told the PIIB that he directed her to destroy documents related to the kickback scam he ran at Vaughn Pharma."

"There's no evidence that he devised the scheme," said Noelle.

"But, the destruction of documents could be problematic for him," said Beanie. "Obstruction of justice is a serious charge. And even if Ted could avoid jail time, the damage to his reputation would be pretty bad."

Noelle stretched out next to Beanie, rolling onto her side, facing him. "The university would probably fire him for breaching the moral turpitude clause."

"Belinda Davenport said he was a millionaire on paper," said Beanie.

"If he loses his job, he won't be able to afford the luxe life in Avalon Estates."

"Guess it's true what they say," said Noelle, propping her elbow on the pillow to rest her head in her palm.

"What's that?" Beanie asked.

"Everyone has secrets, huh?"

"Ted Zamora has more than just secrets," said Beanie, intertwining his fingers with his wife's. "He has a much stronger motive for killing Anna, in my opinion."

Noelle frowned. "You think so?"

"Ted didn't want Anna to tell the PIIB agent about the documents he told her to destroy," said Beanie. "Maybe I should call Octavia Constant. There might be a better suspect, after all."

His wife slipped her fingers from his and turned over onto her back. "I'm not sure about Ted as the killer."

"Belinda said Anna tried to extort money from Ted, which Ted didn't have," Beanie said. "Then Ted suspected that Anna was going to rat him out to the feds. Those are two strong motives for murder."

Noelle sighed. "Okay, maybe Ted did want Anna dead. And I can see him hiring someone to kill her, but I don't think he would have done the deed himself."

"Ted changed his shirt at the egg hunt," said Beanie. "Remember when we were talking to Anna, and then Ted came over and said he had to talk to her right then, it couldn't wait? Ted grabbed Anna and dragged her into the house. When he returned to the party, he was wearing a different shirt."

"I do remember that," said Noelle, rolling onto her side again. "And I remember that Chuck Taylor pointed out that Ted changed his shirt. Ted said he spilled beer on himself and Chuck asked him—"

"He lied to me ..." Beanie sat forward, recalling details of the conversation he'd had with Ted during their first meeting.

"What?"

Beanie stared at his wife. "At the egg hunt, Ted said he spilled beer on himself. But, when I interviewed him after Anna's murder, he told me that Anna tossed a Bloody Mary on him when they were arguing."

Noelle said, "Well, maybe Ted was confused. You talked to him after he'd been interrogated all night."

"He wasn't confused, he was lying," said Beanie. "And he didn't change his shirt because it had Bloody Mary stains. He changed it because there was blood on his shirt ... Anna's blood."

"Hold on, Sherlock," said Noelle, maneuvering to a sitting position.

Beanie frowned. "Sherlock?"

"He's a detective, right?"

"A detective, yeah," said Beanie, chuckling. "Not an investigative reporter."

"Oh, you know what I meant, Roland," said Noelle, smiling. "I just don't think you should jump to conclusions about Ted, especially when there are other things you should consider ..."

"Other things like what?"

His wife glanced away for a moment.

"Noelle?" prodded Beanie.

"Don't think I was trying to step on your toes, because I wasn't," said Noelle, hands lifted as if in surrender. "But, I did a bit of investigating myself."

Beanie laughed. "Well, look at you, Nancy Drew!"

Waving a dismissive hand, Noelle said, "Trust me, I am not about to quit my day job, but—"

"What did you find out?"

"Some of my co-workers from the pharmacy and I went to lunch at Dizzy Jenny's yesterday," said Noelle. "And as I was leaving the ladies' room, I saw Landon George."

Landon George was a waiter at Dizzy Jenny's, an upscale beachfront restaurant popular with tourists and St. Killian residents. Beanie knew George as a reluctant source of information for the *Palmchat Gazette*, specifically when it came to matters involving the PC-5. Though not officially part of the gang, George was a cartel liaison, facilitating transactions for people who needed the gang's services.

"What did he have to say?" asked Beanie, curious about his wife's conversation even though he didn't like the idea of Noelle communicating with anyone associated with the cartel.

"I asked Landon if Anna's and Belinda's boutique had been targeted for the PC-5 protection tax," said Noelle. "Langdon said no about the protection tax, but he told me that something shady is going on at the boutique."

"Something shady like what?"

Noelle said, "Landon didn't know what – or, wasn't will to tell me – but he thinks Anna and Belinda were selling more than custom-made sundresses and matching accessories."

"What else were they selling?"

"Again, Landon didn't know, or wouldn't tell me," said Noelle.

"Drugs, maybe?" asked Beanie.

Noelle said, "That would be my guess..."

22

Officer Fields said, "My friend at the PIIB confirmed that Anna Zamora was speaking to one of their agents."

Beanie had phoned Fields as soon as he'd arrived at the *Palmchat Gazette* offices, a quarter after seven that morning. After a few minutes of small talk, Beanie asked the officer if he knew anything about Anna Zamora contacting the Palmchat Island Investigative Bureau. Despite Ted's plea for discretion, Beanie had thought it prudent to give Fields the details about his conversation with the university president.

Four hours later, Fields returned his call.

"Anna *was* going to turn on Ted," said Beanie, staring at the yellow notepad on his desk. He'd written between the lines another topic he needed to broach with Fields: *Anna and Belinda selling drugs at the boutique?*

Beanie wasn't sure about his wife's theory, though as a former member of the island cartel, she would be in a better position to know if the PC-5 would use a clothing store as a front for trafficking illegal narcotics. Beanie couldn't wrap his head around the idea of the women peddling dope, but he supposed it was possible. From what he'd learned about Anna Zamora, the woman seemed willing to go outside the confines of the law to get what she wanted. After destroying documents that were part of a federal investigation, she'd leveraged her actions to snag a rich husband. When her boutique fell on hard times, she'd resorted to extortion not once, but twice. Still, the drug angle was strange. If Anna and Belinda had been selling drugs, then why was the boutique losing money? Their company should have been flush with cash from drug profits, but they were struggling, near insolvency.

"None of Anna's discussions with the PIIB agent were about her husband, Ted Zamora," said Officer Fields. "My friend wasn't sure why Anna contacted the PIIB. All he knew was that she claimed to have information about criminal activity she felt they needed to be made aware of."

Beanie asked, "Could that criminal activity have been about the trafficking of illegal narcotics?"

"Why do you think that?" asked Fields.

After sharing with Fields the conversation between Noelle and Landon George, Beanie said, "Belinda Davenport told me that Anna was talking to the PIIB about Ted, but maybe not. Maybe Anna and Belinda were using the boutique to sell drugs and got in over their heads. Anna might have thought that the only way to escape would be to inform the feds."

"I'll find out if the boutique was on our radar for any possible illegal drug activity," said Fields. "If so, unfortunately, that's something Janvier would have discounted as having nothing to do with Anna Zamora's death because it doesn't fit with his theory that Delaney Pinkerton killed her."

Beanie shook his head. "How has Janvier not been fired?"

Fields chuckled. "Actually, he does get it right more than he gets it wrong. It's just that when he gets your case wrong, you think he gets every case wrong."

"I guess so," said Beanie, unwilling to concede Fields the point. "Nevertheless, anytime you're dealing with illegal narcotics, there's the probability of somebody getting killed. The PC-5 controls the drug game on the islands. So I have to wonder if Bob Davenport was right. Maybe the PC-5 did have Anna killed."

"And I will look into it, see what I find out," said Fields. "But, remember, Landon George told your wife that something shady was going on at the boutique. So, what's shady? George couldn't tell you. You and Noelle came up with drugs, but what if it's nothing to do with drugs. What if it's firearms? Or, sexual favors? Or, unlicensed medical treatments?"

Beanie sighed. "Like the owner of the adult care center who was busted for offering illegal Botox injections."

"Didn't you write that story?"

"That was another reporter," said Beanie. "But, I get your point."

"Let me get some facts," said Fields. "If I find out there's something to the drug selling angle, I'll bring it to Janvier's attention, and if he doesn't listen, I'll go to the chief."

Following the call with Fields, Beanie made notes from their conversation, and then moved on to fact-checking and making follow-up calls for other stories he was working on. Nothing could distract him from the egg hunt murder, however. He was of the opinion that Delaney Pinkerton was not the killer. The disturbed woman hit Anna with a branch, but she hadn't put a knife in Anna's chest. Ted was crooked and most likely prone to skirt the law, but Noelle was probably right. The university president didn't seem the type to murder someone. The guy was suave and shady, but not sinister enough to shed blood.

Beanie would put his money on the PC-5. His bias against the cartel usually clouded his judgment, but he wasn't accusing the gang just because he hated the organization and blamed it for every type of malfeasance perpetrated on the island.

Landon George was a knowledge source. If he claimed the boutique was dealing in shady business, then it was probably true. Nothing shady happened on the islands without the PC-5 having some part in the shadiness. If Anna and Belinda had engaged in criminal shenanigans, then the PC-5 would have known about it.

Leaning back in his chair, Beanie stroked his jaw.

Was it possible that Anna and Belinda, desperate for money to save their business, came up with a crooked get rich quick scheme, but didn't ask the PC-5 for permission to carry out the scheme? And then maybe the PC-5 threatened Anna, so she went to the PIIB for protection? The PC-5 had moles everywhere, even in the PIIB, and would have learned that Anna went to the Feds. So, then the PC-5 had Anna killed.

Beanie sat forward. Only problem with that scenario was that the PC-5 wouldn't have sent an enforcer to stab Anna. She would have been shot to death. Stabbing was an up close and personal crime. Stabbing victims usually knew their killers, but there were exceptions. An intruder caught by the homeowner might grab a knife, out of convenience, and attack the homeowner.

Shaking his head, Beanie frowned. Though he was leaning toward the PC-5 as being responsible for Anna's death, he might have to rethink his theories if Officer Fields reported that the St. Killian police had no reason to suspect any drug dealing at the boutique.

Beanie glanced at his cell phone. Minutes ago, he'd been thinking of calling Octavia Constant to tell her his speculations about the PC-5, but now he thought he should wait until—

The phone beeped.

Grabbing it, Beanie stared at the screen. A text from Bob Davenport. Curious, Beanie accessed the message:

Can you meet me now. Need your advice! Please. Very important.

Beanie stared at the text. Why would Bob Davenport need his advice? About what? Exhaling, Beanie returned the message, agreeing to meet Bob.

Will be at your place shortly.

23

Driving through the winding roads of Avalon Estates, Beanie couldn't help but think that whoever had coined the phrase "looks can be deceiving" must have had Avalon Estates in mind.

The neighborhood was a stunning community of gorgeous homes nestled within clusters of hibiscus and oleander, but behind the beautiful façade, there was a sinister ugliness. So many secrets were hidden within the enclave of palm-lined streets. The lies were like cancer, spreading and infecting, poisoning and destroying.

Exhaling, Beanie shook his head. In high school, Beanie had a paper route through Avalon Estates. Zipping up and down the streets on his motorbike, he flung copies of the *Palmchat Gazette* toward the ornate double-doored entryways. Envying the upper class, he'd dreamt of one day driving his Mercedes into one of the circular driveways.

Now he wasn't sure he wanted to raise his family among the elite. A spacious home and disposable income might be nice, but not if it came with rampant infidelity, moral erosion, and psychosis.

As Beanie made a right turn, heading down the street toward the Davenport home, his thoughts shifted to the text he'd received from

Bob. What kind of advice did the stay-at-home dad want? And why did he think Beanie was the best person to ask for help?

Making a left into the Davenport driveway, Beanie steered around the circle and parked behind a shiny silver Maserati. He cut the engine of his eight-year-old SUV and was about to exit the vehicle when his phone rang. Staring at the phone, Beanie read the Caller-ID: Pinkerton, Roger.

Beanie groaned. When it rained it poured, he thought as he answered the phone.

"Thank you for taking my call," said the cardiologist. "I won't keep you long."

Promises, promises, thought Beanie, but he said, "No problem. What's going on?"

"I'm concerned about our last conversation," said Roger.

"What's concerning about our last conversation?" asked Beanie, trying to remember what he and Roger had spoken about.

"You told me that Octavia Constant had changed her strategy concerning Delaney's defense," said Roger. "You said I should give her a call, which I did. She told me she wants Delaney to plead guilty by reason of insanity. She wants to show that Delaney was off her medication, which caused her to become psychotic and kill Anna."

Beanie rubbed his eyes. "I take it you don't agree?"

"That's a ridiculous, outrageous, and frankly insulting strategy," said Roger. "And it's not going to work because Delaney took her meds on the day of the egg hunt."

"Delaney told me she didn't take her—"

"My wife is mistaken," said Roger. "Her medication often causes her to forget things. But, I know she took her meds because I watched her take them. Delaney can't be trusted to take her meds on her own, so I monitor her. I make sure she takes them."

"Roger, maybe you should listen to Octavia," suggested Beanie. "She's a great attorney. She knows what she's doing and—"

"I'd like you to call Octavia," said Roger.

"You want me to call Octavia?"

"You have a better relationship with her than I do," said Roger. "She needs to go back to her original strategy: the better suspect. You can convince her to abandon the idea of Delaney pleading guilty because I won't let that happen. I won't risk my wife doing time."

"Delaney might not have to go to jail," said Beanie. "Octavia may be able to get her probation on the condition that she enter the Rakestraw-Blake Center, or—"

"I have an idea of who the better suspect might be," Roger blurted out.

Skeptical, Beanie asked, "You do?"

Roger said, "I've been thinking about it, and I'm sure that—"

Hard slaps against the driver's side window jolted Beanie.

Jerking his head to the left, Beanie cursed.

A hand, palm-side down, hit against the glass, leaving smears of blood ...

24

Beanie's heart plummeted into his stomach and then shot into his throat.

Jerking away from the window, he stared at the bloody handprints. What the hell was happening?

The hand became a fist, beating at the window. "Help! Please help me!"

Forcing himself to focus, Beanie peered through the blood-streaked glass.

Belinda Davenport stood outside his SUV, wailing and crying, begging for help. Beanie opened the door and jumped out of the vehicle.

"I tried to revive him, but he won't wake up!" Belinda screamed, clutching Beanie's shirt, her eyes wild and manic. "He's dead! Bob is dead, and they killed him! They killed him just like they did Anna!"

Confused, his mind buzzing with questions, Beanie grabbed Belinda and shook her. "Calm down and tell me what happened to Bob!"

"They shot him!"

"Who shot him?"

"The PC-5!" Belinda yelled, bursting into heaving sobs.

"The PC-5 shot Bob?" asked Beanie, his confusion increasing. "When? Where is he?"

"He's in the house!" Belinda shrieked, shaking violently.

Worried that she might collapse, Beanie put an arm around her and dragged her along as he strode toward the house.

"Where is Bob?" Beanie asked, focused on the ornate double doors of the Davenport home, one of which was opened.

"Kitchen," gasped Belinda. "He's in the kitchen! I came home, and I found him on the floor!"

"And the girls?" Beanie asked as they crossed the threshold and headed into the foyer. "Where are they?"

"The girls?" Belinda rasped. "Ballet. No. Gymnastics. They're at gymnastics practice! Oh, God! My girls! My precious little sweethearts—"

"Where is the kitchen?" Beanie asked, supporting Belinda as they hurried down the hall.

Belinda guided him, and after several turns down several more hallways, they reached the large kitchen, a bright room anchored by a huge rectangular island. Bamboo wood cabinetry mixed with commercial grade appliances, creating a chic, tropical atmosphere.

"He's over there!" Belinda pointed toward the island. "Oh, God, Bob! Oh, my God!"

Herding Belinda over to a round table in the breakfast nook, Beanie pulled out a chair and forced the distraught designer to sit.

"Did you call 911?" Beanie asked.

Eyes wide, Belinda stared at him. "What? 911? No. I saw Bob lying on the floor, bleeding, and I tried to help him, but—"

"Call 911!" Beanie ordered, rushing toward the island. Walking around the large slab of beige marble, Beanie found Bob lying in the six-foot space between the island and the counter that housed the kitchen sink. Afternoon sunlight slanted through the French doors, casting a coppery glow over Bob's prone form. Beanie dropped to one knee next to the stay-at-home dad, trying to assess his injuries.

"Bob! Can you hear me?" Beanie stared at the large, dark red bloodstain spread across Bob's light-colored polo shirt. From his days working the Handweg crime beat, Beanie guessed that Bob had been shot in the chest.

"My husband has been shot!" Belinda shouted. "Please come now! He's lost a lot of blood!"

His heart slamming, Beanie pressed two fingers against Bob's neck. "Tell the dispatcher that his pulse is very weak!"

Belinda relayed the message and then said, "They want to know if he's breathing!"

Glancing over his shoulder, Beanie stared at Belinda, standing a few feet behind him, a cordless phone pressed against the side of her face. "Barely."

"He's barely breathing!" Belinda said to the dispatcher. "Come now, please!"

As Belinda recited the address to the home, Beanie stared at Bob. Eyes closed and mouth slack, the man was ashen and appeared lifeless. Beanie said a quick prayer. "Stay with us, Bob. Fight, man. Your girls need you."

"The ambulance is coming," said Belinda.

Nodding, Beanie said, "Get a dishcloth. We need to apply pressure to the wound."

Seconds later, Belinda kneeled in front of her husband's head and thrust a rag toward Beanie.

"Did the dispatcher give you an ETA?" asked Beanie, folding the cloth into fourths before he placed it on Bob's chest and pressed down.

"They'll be here as soon as possible," cried Belinda. "Oh, God, he can't die! He just can't!"

"Explain to me what happened," Beanie said, disturbed by the blood soaking into the dish towel.

"I told you, I came home, and I found him like this!" Belinda said. "He'd been shot, and he was bleeding!"

"He was conscious when you first found him?" Beanie stared at her.

Belinda nodded. "He was gasping for breath and wheezing. I told him not to talk, to save his strength, but he wanted to tell me what happened."

"And that's when he told you the PC-5 had shot him?"

Nodding again, Belinda said, "They tried to kill him, just like they killed Anna!"

"Why did you run out of the house?" Beanie asked, hoping his questions would stop Belinda from getting hysterical.

Belinda shook her head. "I don't know, I—"

"Was the gunman still in the house?"

"I don't know," said Belinda. "No. I don't think so … I left the house to get help from my neighbor."

"Help from your neighbor?" Beanie tried to keep the skepticism from his tone, but as Belinda looked away, he knew she'd picked up on his suspicion of her behavior. Most of the homes in Avalon Estates sat on two acres of land. Her nearest neighbor was probably about ten minutes away.

"I should have immediately called an ambulance," said Belinda. "But, I panicked."

Beanie wasn't sure if he believed her, or not, but he supposed that seeing her husband bleeding on the floor could have robbed her of the ability to think clearly and rationally.

"Do you hear that?" asked Belinda.

Beanie focused, listening.

Sirens, faint at first, grew louder.

"That's the ambulance!" Belinda jumped up. "I'll show them into the kitchen."

25

"What did Belinda Davenport tell you?" Beanie asked Officer Fields, who stood near the elevator vestibule on the ground level of St. Killian General Hospital.

Moments ago, the policeman had wrapped up his questioning of the designer, an exchange which had taken place in the waiting room, a spacious area decorated in soothing, calm hues of soft blue and mint green. From his seat in a row of chairs a few feet from Belinda and Fields, Beanie watched with covert interest. Fields seemed patient and compassionate, while the designer alternated between hysteria and catatonia. Beanie had been respectful, giving Fields the space he needed to conduct his investigation. As soon as the officer stood and headed away from Belinda, Beanie jumped up, eager to talk with Fields before the man left.

Fields turned his head slightly. Beanie followed the officer's eyes to Belinda Davenport, sitting on a loveseat in a corner near a wide rectangular window overlooking the small, man-made lake behind the hospital.

"Pretty much the same thing she told you," said Fields. "She came home early to have lunch with her husband only to find him on the floor in the kitchen bleeding from a gunshot wound. She tried to revive him, and when she couldn't, she ran out of the house, intending to get help from a neighbor."

"What do you think about her story?" Beanie asked, staring at Belinda. Her head turned toward the window, she hugged herself as she slowly rocked back and forth.

Fields made a face. "I do find it strange that she didn't think to call an ambulance, but some people are irrational when it comes to stressful situations. I'm more concerned about her assertion that a member of the PC-5 shot her husband."

"You believe her?" asked Beanie.

Fields stared at him. "Unlike Janvier, I'm not going to rush to judgment before I get all the facts. I need to make some phone calls. Talk to some people who might be able to corroborate her story."

"Which part?"

"She claims that the PC-5 shot her husband because the cartel wanted protection tax from the boutique, but she didn't have the money to pay it," said Fields. "She claims the gang killed her business partner, Anna Zamora, for the same reason, because they couldn't pay the protection tax."

Stunned, Beanie gaped at Fields. "A few days ago, I spoke to Bob Davenport, and he told me the PC-5 had killed Anna Zamora for refusing to pay the protection tax. When I asked Belinda about it, she swore up and down that Bob was wrong. She claimed that Ted had killed Anna."

Fields said, "That's interesting. But as I said, I'm not rushing to judgment. I have a lot to sort out, but I'll tell you this. If I find out that the boutique wasn't targeted for the protection tax, then Mrs. Davenport and I are going to have another conversation, and she's going to tell me the truth—or else."

After Officer Fields left, Beanie walked back to the waiting room and took the chair adjacent to Belinda.

"Have you heard anything about Bob's condition?" asked Beanie.

Belinda looked at him with watery, red-rimmed eyes. Sniffing, she rubbed a crumpled tissue beneath her nose, and said, "He's still in surgery. The doctors told me that the bullet didn't damage any major organs, but he lost so much blood and … oh, God, what am I going to do if Bob doesn't make it?"

"Don't think like that," said Beanie, reaching for her hand, then squeezing it. "Keep praying and staying positive. Bob's going to make it."

"He has to make it," said Belinda. "My girls can't lose their father. They're crazy about Bob. They'll be devastated if—"

"Where are the girls?" asked Beanie.

"I have an au pair who helps Bob," said Belinda, blowing her nose. "I called her. She picked the girls up from gymnastics and took them home with her. The girls can spend the night with her so that I can stay here with Bobby."

Nodding, Beanie said, "Good. Glad to hear that."

"I told Celeste, the au pair, to tell the girls that daddy and I are at dinner," said Belinda. "I have to tell them, but not right now. I'm a mess, and I don't want to scare the girls."

"Probably would be better to talk to them tomorrow," said Beanie, pulling his hand away. "Bob will be out of surgery and maybe even able to receive visitors."

"God, I hope so," said Belinda, nodding. "I hope so."

Beanie cleared his throat. "I saw you talking to Officer Fields."

Belinda stared at him, her expression blank.

"Did he tell you if the cops have any leads on who shot Bob?"

Shaking her head, Belinda said, "I already know who shot Bob. I told Officer Fields. It was the PC-5. Whether he believed me, or not, I don't know, but I told him the police need to leave Delaney alone. The PC-5 killed Anna, and they shot Bob."

"Because you and Anna wouldn't pay the PC-5 protection tax?" Beanie asked.

Belinda nodded.

"A few days ago, when we talked, I asked you about the protection tax, and you said—"

"I lied, okay," said Belinda, shaking her head. "I had no choice. I couldn't risk you writing about it in the *Palmchat Gazette* and having the PC-5 come after me and my family, but they came anyway. They shot Bob, and it's all my fault. It should have been me bleeding on that floor!"

"Don't say that," said Beanie.

"But, it's true," said Belinda, tears streaming down her cheeks. "The PC-5 wasn't after Bob. My husband was in the wrong place at the wrong time. The cartel came to kill me."

26

"Bob made it through the surgery," said Noelle, placing her cell phone on the nightstand next to the king-sized bed.

"Was that Belinda?" asked Beanie.

Climbing on the bed, Noelle shook her head. "Florence Taylor. The doctors think he's going to make it, but they moved him to ICU to monitor his condition overnight."

"Thank God," said Beanie, exhaling as he leaned back on the pillows against the headboard.

A long, horrible, confusing day was finally coming to an end. Knowing that Bob had survived the surgery, Beanie felt he could relax, and wouldn't be up half the night, worrying and wondering, replaying the events of the afternoon.

Beanie hadn't wanted to leave Belinda alone at the hospital, but Vivian—who'd heard about the shooting from another reporter who'd been monitoring the police scanners—had wanted him to write about Bob's shooting. Beanie was reluctant. Vivian felt that the second instance of violent crime in Avalon Estates, a neighborhood seen as the last place where violent crimes occurred, warranted prominent placement in the paper. Beanie's connection to both victims made the story more intriguing and interesting. Once again, Beanie had been an up close, and personal eye witness and the paper had to take advantage of that.

After writing a quick dispatch of pertinent facts for the paper's online version, Beanie headed home. Driving to Oyster Farms, he'd called Noelle to update her on the tragic events.

Noelle said, "I can't imagine how devastated the girls would have been if Bob had died."

Beanie shared his wife's sentiments about the Davenport girls. Losing their father would have destroyed them.

"Belinda must have been going out of her mind," said Noelle.

"That might explain why she didn't think to call an ambulance when she found Bob bleeding on the floor of their kitchen," said Beanie.

"I know it's crazy to think that 911 wouldn't have been her first thought," said Noelle. "But, you don't know what it's like to see someone you love with a life-threatening injury. You can't think. There's just panic. And confusion. That's how it was for me when you were stabbed."

"Babe, don't think about that," said Beanie, reaching to grab his wife's hand.

"I can't help it," said Noelle. "Hearing about Belinda finding Bob took me right back to that moment—"

"Don't go back there."

"Roland, you could have died," said Noelle, eyes glistening with unshed tears. "The boys and I could have lost you."

"But, you didn't," said Beanie, not in the mood to revisit that awful day when a crazed psycho had plunged a knife into his chest. "I made it through. And so has Bob."

"Belinda must be so relieved," said Noelle.

"Yeah," said Beanie, though he wasn't sure Belinda had felt relief when she'd found out that her husband had survived his gunshot wound, but he kept his opinions to himself. Beanie was suspicious of Belinda, but he didn't know why. He couldn't articulate the reason for his doubt about the designer, but her conflicting, changing stories bothered him. First, she'd sworn that the PC-5 hadn't targeted the boutique for their protection tax. Then, she admitted that the boutique had been targeted, but she'd been forced to lie to protect her family.

"I can't believe the PC-5 shot Bob," said Noelle.

Beanie stared at his wife, curious about her tone. Had he heard hints of astonishment? Or skepticism?

"Neither can I," said Beanie.

"You sound like you don't believe the PC-5 shot him because you think someone else did," said Noelle.

"I was going to say the same thing about you," said Beanie. "Is there a specific reason why you can't believe that the PC-5 killed Bob?"

Noelle sighed. "When the gang sends someone after you, it's you they go after. Vadaj never misses its mark. If they'd sent an enforcer to shoot Belinda, that enforcer would not have shot Bob because Belinda wasn't home. The enforcers do their due diligence. They know how to hunt the target they've been assigned to take down."

Beanie asked, "Any chance it could have been an inexperienced enforcer?"

Noelle shook her head. "I doubt it. Enforcers go through rigorous training – first as an apprentice, then as an assistant, before getting assignments. They usually hit their targets."

"So, if the PC-5 shot Bob, then it was because he was the target."

"Right," said Noelle. "But why target Bob?"

"Bob texted me because he wanted advice about something," said Beanie. "That's why I was at the house. Maybe he wanted advice about ratting on the PC-5. He did tell me the gang killed Anna. Snitching would make him a target."

Noelle said, "Bob isn't stupid. He knows you can't rat on the gang."

Beanie said, "Maybe that's why he wanted advice. How to snitch without getting stitches? Bob told me that Belinda wanted him to stay quiet about the protection tax, but maybe he wanted to tell the cops."

Noelle asked, "Who do you think shot Bob? Because I know you don't think it was the PC-5."

Rubbing his jaw, Beanie said, "I'm not sure ..."

"Roland," said Noelle, giving him a dubious side-eye.

His wife knew he was lying, which was true, but Beanie was reluctant to voice his theories, which were based only on his gut, not any rational speculation.

"I think someone was trying to silence Bob," said Beanie, pulling Noelle into his arms. "Whoever shot him wanted to make sure he couldn't tell what he knows about Anna's death."

"So, you think ..."

"I think Bob was shot because he knows who really killed Anna."

27

"Bob Davenport is lying to me," said Officer Damon Fields.

"When did you talk to him?" asked Beanie, grabbing a pen and a Steno pad to jot down details from the conversation, which Beanie had tried to have yesterday. Beanie had called Fields to get a quote for his follow-up to PC-5 TARGETS AVALON ESTATES RESIDENT, but the officer had been too busy to speak with him.

Since the attempt on his life three days ago, Bob had steadily improved, even quicker than doctors expected, and was on track to make a complete recovery.

"I went to the hospital this morning," said Fields. "Janvier flew to the Aerie Islands last night, so he asked me to take Davenport's statement since the doctors cleared him to be questioned."

"Why do you think Bob is lying to you?" asked Beanie, scribbling a reminder to ask Fields about Janvier's trip to the Aerie Islands.

"Davenport claims he's got amnesia," grumbled Fields.

"Amnesia?" echoed Beanie, shocked.

"Can't remember shit, to hear him tell it," said Fields. "Doesn't remember being shot, which I find highly suspicious. A bullet to the chest is hard to forget."

"His entire memory is gone?"

"Not everything. Just the events surrounding the shooting," said Fields. "He can't remember the things we need to know to investigate the case and catch the perp. Was hoping Davenport could describe the shooter, but …"

"And you think he's faking the amnesia?"

Fields said, "His doctors said he didn't suffer any traumatic brain injury. There's no medical or physical reason for the memory loss. Bob claims the last thing he remembers is dropping off his girls at gymnastics around noon, which I confirmed. I'm still working on the timeline of events, though."

"Maybe it's psychological," suggested Beanie, though he didn't believe that. "Amnesia brought on by emotional trauma. Sometimes people will block out traumatic events."

"And sometimes, people will pretend to have no memory of an event because they're hiding something."

Or, protecting someone, thought Beanie, deciding to keep his opinions to himself.

Beanie asked, "What do you think he's hiding? You think he knows who shot him?"

"Damn right, he does," said Fields. "And he knows why he was shot, too. He just doesn't want to tell us."

"Why wouldn't he want the person who shot him arrested?"

"I think he's afraid of retribution," said Fields. "I checked out what you told me about something shady going on at the boutique, and I think you're right, though I haven't been able to confirm or deny anything. Seems everybody has amnesia these days, but somebody will crack, eventually."

Beanie agreed. From his days working the Handweg beat, he knew that low-level thugs would quickly spill their guts, offering details about unsolved crimes, in exchange for prosecutorial leniency.

"Before you go," said Beanie, staring at the reminder on the yellow pad. "Why did Janvier go to the Aerie Islands?"

"The Rakestraw-Blake Center got the results back on the sweat DNA yesterday," said Fields.

"Was it a match for Delaney Pinkerton?" asked Beanie, recalling the plastic glove covered in Anna Zamora's blood that had been found buried in the bottom of the trash can at the Zamora home.

"You can mention this in your story, but you didn't hear it from me …"

"Of course," said Beanie.

"The sweat DNA wasn't a match for Janvier's main suspect," said Fields. "Janvier went to meet with detectives in Amargo. They're going to run the DNA through their island-wide databases, which contain information on criminals across the entire Caribbean, from the Bahamas to Trinidad."

"How'd Janvier take the news?" asked Beanie.

Fields chuckled. "He thinks they may have gotten the results wrong, which is another reason why he's flying there. He wants them to test Delaney Pinkerton again."

"Why am I not surprised," said Beanie.

Fields said, "I don't think Janvier is going to get the results he wants, but I do think he might find out who really killed Anna Zamora."

28

"You got the story wrong," said the debonair, dubious man Beanie knew only as "Lime Shoes," an old gangster with a long tenure in the PC-5.

Sitting at a booth against the wall in a secluded corner, his normal spot, the gangster ran his finger around the rim of a small glass of amber liquid sitting on a square napkin. Wearing his customary white dress shirt opened at the collar, revealing a necklace made of shark's teeth, and a white Panama Jack straw hat, he motioned for Beanie to sit across from him on the cracked leather bench seat.

Seconds later, a waiter ambled over, and Beanie ordered a Felipe beer. Close to calling it a day, Beanie had been working on revisions to articles, fact-checking, and making phone calls when he received the text from Lime Shoes, who'd requested a meeting at the Purple Gecko, a seedy bar in Handweg Gardens known as a PC-5 hangout.

Almost a year had passed since he'd last heard from the old gangster —which was a good thing. A call from Lime Shoes was always a cause for concern, even though Beanie usually ended up with behind the scenes details for his articles.

Staring at the PC-5 veteran, Beanie reflected on the first time he'd met the man. Six years ago, before Beanie had met Noelle, he'd been a junior beat reporter, two years on the job, covering crime. Beanie had written a story about a 90-year-old great grandmother who'd been killed during the robbery of a Handweg grocery store. His article had placed the blame on PC-5 *Pescado*, or fish, fresh thugs new to the gang. Newbie PC-5 members sometimes, to prove their worth to the gang, would be overzealous in their criminal exploits, and innocent people would get caught in the crossfire.

Beanie's story had been lauded by his editors as damn good journalism. Incensed and inspired, the residents of Handweg had protested the gang's violence, which often went ignored and unchecked by the police. Beanie had been feeling proud about his work, when one day, on his way home, he'd been ambushed by three guys who pulled guns on him and hustled him into the back of a car. Praying he wouldn't be shot in the head, Beanie spent the ride in a blind panic, trying not to shit on himself. Finally, after careening down several dark, twisting roads, the vehicle pulled up to a small, dilapidated shanty house surrounded by tropical rainforest.

Shoved into the house, Beanie was pushed down into a chair at a rickety card table in a humid kitchen.

Sitting across from him was a fifty-something man who introduced himself as Lime Shoes.

"You know why you're here?" Lime Shoes had asked, head tilted, his gaze circumspect.

Unable to find his voice, Beanie shook his head.

Lime Shoes proceeded to tell him the cartel was upset about a story he'd written.

"You got the facts wrong in your story about that old woman," said Lime Shoes. "You need to get the story right. The PC-5 don't appreciate being associated with the killing of a great-grandmother. I'm going to give you the correct details so you can print a retraction. Consider it a favor from me to you, because I like your writing style."

"Thanks ..." Beanie mumbled, eyes darting from the old man in front of him to the thugs flanking him, brandishing guns.

"Piece of advice, young man," said Lime Shoes. "When it comes to stories about the PC-5, make sure your facts are right. Don't ever accuse the gang of something they had nothing to do with."

Beanie nodded, not trusting himself to speak.

Lime Shoes said, "I realize that might be a challenge, so I'll help you out if you make a mistake, so you can get things straight."

Since that fateful meeting, Lime Shoes had been an unofficial source, someone Beanie could count on to help him get the details right when he wrote about the PC-5.

"What story did I get wrong this time?" Beanie asked, staring at the man.

"PC-5 didn't have shit to do with that murder in Fantasy Land."

Fantasy Land, Beanie knew, was what Handweg residents called Avalon Estates. A derogatory term, Fantasy Land referred to the reality that for Handweg citizens, living in Avalon Estates was an unattainable pipe dream. Avalon Estates residents were seen as living insulated in paradise from the violent crime and economic disenfranchisement those in Handweg suffered.

"It wasn't a Vadaj hit?" asked Beanie, his tone skeptical even though he believed Lime Shoes. The more he ruminated on the events surrounding Bob's attempted murder, the more Beanie was convinced that the cartel had nothing to do with it, despite Bob's assertions that the PC-5 had killed Anna Zamora because she refused to pay the protection tax.

Lime Shoes took a sip of his drink, then said, "You know Vadaj don't miss."

Beanie nodded. He'd heard rumors that Vadaj enforcers and assassins didn't miss because they *couldn't* miss. Missing a target meant becoming a target. Vadaj employed a "kill or be killed" policy that was strictly upheld. Beanie took a sip of beer. "You know anything about who put those bullets in his chest?"

"Don't know who shot that man in Fantasy Land," said Lime Shoes. "Ain't my concern. What I know is that if he knew what I know and he wanted to talk about what he knew, then somebody might want to shut him up, stop him from talking."

"What do you know?"

"Nothing I want to see in the papers."

"Between you and me," promised Beanie.

Lime Shoes gave Beanie a shrewd look.

"You know you can trust me," said Beanie.

Lime Shoes said, "What I know is that there is rumored to be an unauthorized operation at the boutique owned by the wife of the man who was shot."

Beanie frowned. In PC-5 speak, an unauthorized operation was a criminal endeavor taking place without the gang's permission. The PC-5 wasn't responsible for all crime across the Palmchat Islands, but any unlawful enterprise was subject to their approval and permission. No criminal could set up shop in the Palmchat Islands without making sure the PC-5 sanctioned the operation. Permission always required an initial start-up fee and subsequent payments for protection and autonomy. Criminals who dared to ignore the cartel's rules faced swift retribution.

"You know any details about the unauthorized operation?" asked Beanie.

"Fancy designer drugs," said Lime Shoes. "CBC oils. Shit you sell to rich tourists at the Queen Palm."

"Who's running the operation?" asked Beanie.

"Lady who got stabbed in Fantasy Land at that Easter egg hunt," said the old gangster.

"Anna Zamora?"

"Don't know what her name was," said Lime Shoes. "Just know she was doing something she ain't had no business doing without permission."

Flabbergasted, Beanie shook his head. "Was she running the operation with her business partner?"

"Don't know about that," Lime Shoes said. "Maybe. Maybe not. I know she had a crew of castoffs working for her."

Castoffs were wanna-be gang members who'd tried to join the cartel but couldn't meet the rigorous, deadly demands of thug life. Not everyone was cut out for the PC-5, Beanie had learned—ironically, from Lime Shoes. Much like the military, the cartel recruited those with the best possibility of success. Qualifications for joining the PC-5 had changed dramatically under the new, third-generation leadership.

The original members and the succession, the second-generation, welcomed anyone willing to pledge allegiance to the cartel. That changed when the third generation took over several years ago and decided to structure the PC-5 as though it was a Fortune-500 conglomerate. Now, prospective gang members had to profess interest by applying, and then proving their worth through either cunning slyness, unabashed brutality, or treacherous intelligence. Acceptance was not guaranteed. Those cast aside were referred to as castoffs, a dishonorable distinction.

After another sip of beer, Beanie said, "Something doesn't make sense. Don't castoffs know better than to get involved in an unauthorized operation?"

Lime Shoes nodded. "Most castoffs end up working for the gang anyway. They're runners. Lookouts. Eyes and ears. But, a few of them want to prove to the cartel that they shouldn't have been cast aside. So, they'll risk pulling some scheme, hoping the gang will give them another chance."

"You know which castoffs she hired?" Beanie asked.

Lime Shoes smiled at him, revealing a gold tooth with a diamond in its center. "I happen to have that information."

29

"You still thinking of having Delaney Pinkerton plead guilty because of insanity?" Beanie asked Octavia Constant when the attorney answered his call. "Or, are you willing to consider a better suspect?"

"The sweat DNA doesn't match my client," said Octavia, "which makes it highly unlikely that she stabbed Anna Zamora to death, so I'm thinking of revisiting my tried-and-true strategy."

Leaning back in his chair, Beanie put his feet up on the edge of his desk. "That might be a good idea."

Octavia said, "Care to explain why?"

Beanie recounted the conversation he'd had with Lime Shoes yesterday.

"Interesting," said Octavia.

Leaning an elbow on his desk, Beanie pressed the speaker button on his phone and lowered the volume.

"Noelle and I talked about it last night. If Lime Shoes was right," said Beanie, "and Anna used the boutique for malfeasance without permission from the cartel, then the PC-5 would have to teach her a lesson."

Octavia said, "Makes sense because Anna didn't know how the gang worked. She probably didn't know about the permission rule. Anna might have been approached by the gang and told the error of her ways. Maybe she hadn't taken the gang seriously? So, they killed her."

Beanie said, "Bob Davenport told me that the PC-5 killed Anna, but I don't think he was right."

Scoffing, Octavia said, "Why not? Because some guy named Lime Shoes told you the gang had nothing to do with Anna's murder?"

"I believe him," said Beanie. "I think Anna was killed by one of the castoffs she was working with."

"How do you figure that?"

"I think Anna agreed to work with the castoffs because she needed the money to save the boutique," said Beanie. "But, then she got in over her head, so she decided to rat on the castoffs, which was why she was in contact with the PIIBs."

"Wait. Anna was talking to the PIIBs?"

"I thought I told you that," said Beanie, then went on to bring Octavia up to date. "So, when the castoffs found out that Anna was getting ready to snitch on them, they killed her."

"So why was Bob shot?"

"I think he found out about Anna's deal with the castoffs," said Beanie. "I think he was going to the cops, so they broke into the Davenport house and shot him, which makes sense because a Vadaj enforcer would have killed Bob. Whoever shot Bob wasn't a pro."

"You have the names of the castoff who were working with Anna, right?" asked Octavia. "Have you talked to them?"

"Haven't even found them yet," said Beanie, rubbing his jaw. "And I'm swamped at work. Don't really have time to look, but I think they are the key to solving this murder."

"You know who could find these guys? Ish," said Octavia, using the nickname for her cousin, Icarus Ishmael, who did investigative work for her.

"Roger Pinkerton said he doesn't work for you anymore," said Beanie. "Why is that?"

Octavia sighed. "He's just having some challenges, which is such a shame because things were going so well for him and his wife, Quinn."

"I didn't know he'd gotten married," said Beanie.

"Last year," said Octavia. "Everything was great. They were so in love and thinking of starting a family, but then Ish developed PTSD."

"PTSD?"

"You don't really know the history of him and Quinn," said Octavia, "and it's a long, long story full of murder and mayhem, but Quinn was attacked, and Ish was stabbed trying to save her."

"Sounds familiar," said Beanie, trying not to revisit the moment when a blade had pierced his chest.

"Ish turned to alcohol to cope and wouldn't let Quinn help him," said Octavia. "Six months ago, she went to Houston to help her dad with a case and decided she was going to stay there."

"Is Icarus going to join her in the States?"

"I doubt it," said Octavia. "A month ago, Quinn told Ish she wanted a divorce."

"I hate to hear that," said Beanie.

"Ish went on a bender and ended up in a bad car accident that he's still recovering from," said Octavia. "I put my foot down and forced him to check into the Rakestraw-Blake Center. He enrolled in their 90-day substance abuse program, so that's why he's not working for me."

"I'm glad he's getting help," said Beanie.

After a pause, Octavia asked, "How did you handle it?"

"What?"

"When you were stabbed," said Octavia. "Did you have any issues?"

"Not really …" said Beanie, glancing at his wedding photo. "For me, it was a situation where I was trying to save Noelle, so if I had to take a knife to the chest, then fine. Anything to make sure nothing bad happened to my wife."

"You really would die for her, wouldn't you?" asked Octavia, a wistfulness in her soft tone.

"Yeah, I really would," said Beanie, focusing on Noelle's image in the wedding pic. "But, I have to tell you, I'm so grateful and thankful that I didn't have to …"

30

"Not disturbing family time, am I?" asked Officer Damon Fields.

"Actually, I'm missing family time," admitted Beanie, pressing the speaker button on his desk phone. "I'm still at work."

"Doing what?" asked Fields. "It's after nine o'clock."

"Working on a story," said Beanie, remembering his conversation yesterday with Lime Shoes. "Trying to get it right."

Most of his colleagues had left for the day, but Beanie had decided to stick around and develop a different angle to the story about Bob's attempted murder. An angle that shifted the blame from the PC-5 and to the real culprits—the castoffs who'd worked the unauthorized operation with Anna Zamora. According to Lime Shoes, the would-be gang members were brothers named Lanny and Hugh Gris.

"Well, I won't keep you long," said Fields. "I need to ask you something. Need your help clearing up some things for me."

"I'll try," said Beanie, leaning back in his chair.

"I've been working on the timeline of events regarding the Bob Davenport case," said Fields. "I've come across several inconsistencies."

Grabbing a pad and pen, Beanie wrote: *Timeline – Bob's attempted murder.*

Fields said, "On the day of the incident, at 12:13 pm, Davenport dropped his daughters off at gymnastics class, which I've been able to confirm with the instructor and several other witnesses. At 12:47 pm, Davenport drove downtown to his wife's boutique on Fish Market Way. At 1:09 pm, Davenport and his wife went to lunch at Dizzy Jenny's which I was able to confirm with witnesses and the credit card Davenport used to pay for the meal. At 1:53 pm, Davenport and his wife drove to their home on Sandy Shell Lane, which I confirmed from the alarm system and exterior surveillance. At 2:21 pm, Davenport sent you a text message."

Beanie said, "He wanted my advice."

"About what?"

"I have no idea," said Beanie. "I drove to his house to meet with him, but ..."

"The exterior camera surveillance shows you arriving at 3:06 pm."

Beanie wrote the time of his arrival on his notepad. He couldn't remember what time he'd turned into the Davenport's circular driveway, but three o'clock sounded about right.

"At 3:11 pm, Belinda Davenport ran out of the house and toward your car. She banged on the window. You got out of the car. The two of you spoke and then entered the house."

"That's what happened," said Beanie.

"What did you and Belinda Davenport talk about when she ran out to your car?" asked Fields.

"Belinda was hysterical," said Beanie, recalling the gruesome moment. "I was trying to get her to calm down and tell me what happened."

"And she told you...?"

"She said Bob had been shot," Beanie said. "Belinda told me she came home and ... wait a minute, something's not right."

Fields said, "What's not right is Belinda Davenport's story. I reviewed the statement you gave me, which was that Belinda Davenport told you that she came home and found her husband bleeding on the kitchen floor. Is that still how you remember it?"

Beanie sat forward. "Absolutely. Belinda told me that she came home and found Bob."

"That's what she told me at the hospital," said Fields. "She said that she went to work, then drove home. She said she arrived at the house around two o'clock. She went into the kitchen and found her husband lying on the floor from a gunshot wound to his chest."

"How could Bob have sent me a text at 2:21," said Beanie, glancing at the notes he'd made, "if, at 2 pm, he was bleeding on the kitchen floor?"

"That's what I want to know," said Fields. "Another question is, how did Belinda Davenport drive home from work and find Bob around two o'clock if they arrived at their house together at two o'clock? And if, as Belinda Davenport claims, the PC-5 shot Bob, how did the shooter get into the house? The camera surveillance doesn't show any intruders breaking into the home."

"Did you talk to Belinda about the inconsistencies?"

Fields scoffed. "Mrs. Davenport claims that she got confused about the timing. She admitted to going to lunch with her husband and says they drove home together."

"So, she was in the house when the gunmen broke in and shot Bob?"

"She claims that when they got home, they engaged in marital duties, and then she took a shower. Alone. She says Bob left the bedroom. After her shower, she went to the kitchen and found Bob. She claims she didn't hear any gunshots. She also informed me that they don't have cameras around the entire exterior, so it's possible the shooter entered the home in one of the blind spots."

"What do you think of her story?" asked Beanie.

"I think it's bullshit," said Fields. "I think Belinda Davenport shot her husband. Now, I just have to prove it."

31

Belinda Davenport shot her husband.

Officer Fields' theory rang in Beanie's head, annoying and intrusive, making it impossible to get any work done. Rubbing a hand along his jaw, Beanie glanced around the empty newsroom. Everyone had gone home, and the place was dim and quiet.

Beanie couldn't wrap his head around Fields' accusation, though not because it was unfounded. Fields had made good points. Belinda's inconsistencies were disturbing and glaring. She'd lied to Fields. But, Beanie wasn't ready to convince himself that she was a murderer.

First of all, he couldn't imagine why Belinda would shoot Bob? Why would she try to kill her husband? From what Beanie had observed, they seemed to have a good marriage, but ...

Grabbing a pen, Beanie made doodles across the lined paper. A memory had sparked within him. At the egg hunt, Bob and Belinda had argued. Beanie recalled Chuck pointing out their heated discussion. But, so what? They'd argued. Beanie didn't know a married couple who didn't argue. To say that an argument at an egg hunt had led to attempted murder was slippery slope logic.

Then again, Beanie supposed it depended on what Bob and Belinda had been arguing about.

Beanie's cell phone beeped.

He accessed the text message. Noelle wrote: *just finished my class and heading to mom's to get the boys. Can you start dinner? We should be home in an hour or so.*

Beanie replied: *Still at work but will pick up something.*

After confirming Noelle's agreement, Beanie powered down his computer. He was thinking of stopping at a local late-night roadside food truck for jerk goat, which the boys loved, but he wanted to make another stop first. He wanted to get the truth behind Belinda's lies. The designer might be willing to be more forthcoming with him than she would with the police. Beanie wondered if the castoffs, Lanny and Hugh Gris, were forcing Belinda to continue running the unauthorized operation they'd started with Anna Zamora. Belinda might have been lying to protect herself and her family. Lies of self-preservation, thought Beanie. Belinda and Bob might have argued about working with the castoffs. Bob might have wanted to tell the police, but maybe Belinda didn't want to take the risk, knowing how dangerous the castoffs were.

Standing, Beanie glanced at his watch. 8:16 pm. Belinda Davenport's boutique closed at nine and was only twenty minutes from the *Palmchat Gazette* offices. He had plenty of time to head there before the designer left the shop for the night.

Fifteen minutes later, standing behind the cash wrap counter, Belinda Davenport said, "I don't have time to talk right now. I'm closing up."

"In thirty minutes," said Beanie, refusing to be denied. "I won't take up too much of your time."

"I hope you won't," said Belinda. "I need to pick up the girls and stop by the hospital to see Bob before visiting hours are over."

"How is Bob?" asked Beanie.

"Better every day," said Belinda, her smile tight. "What did you want to talk to me about?"

"Lanny and Hugh Gris," said Beanie, deciding to forgo subtlety and get right to the point.

Belinda stared at him for a moment and then turned toward the cash register. Stabbing keys, she asked, "Who are Lanny and Hugh Gris?"

"PC-5 castoffs," said Beanie.

Punching more keys, Belinda shook her head. "Why are you asking me about PC-5 castoffs?"

"Lanny Gris, or maybe his brother, Hugh," said Beanie, "might have had something to do with Anna's murder. One of them might have also shot Bob."

The cash register made several beeping noises.

"What makes you think that?" asked Belinda, staring at the register's 5x7 horizontal screen.

"One of my sources told me that the Gris brothers were running an unauthorized operation with Anna Zamora," said Beanie. "I think Anna was killed because she was going to snitch on the Gris brothers to the PIIB."

A long piece of thin register tape slid out from a slit near the top of the machine.

Yanking the tape from the register, Belinda shook her head. "I told you that the PC-5 killed Anna and they shot Bob—"

"I don't think that's true," said Beanie. "First of all, the PC-5 wouldn't have stabbed Anna. You know that's not the M.O. of a Vadaj enforcer. Second, as my source pointed out to me, Vadaj don't miss. Bob would be dead if the PC-5 targeted him for murder."

Belinda glared at him. "You didn't tell the cops this stupid theory about the Gris brothers, did you?"

Thrown by the question, Beanie asked, "What if I did?"

"You don't need to send the police on some wild-goose chase," said Belinda. "The police need to focus on the PC-5. That's who killed Anna and shot Bob."

"Are the Gris brothers forcing you to work with them?" asked Beanie.

"What are you talking about?"

"You know they killed Anna because she was going to expose the operation, don't you?" asked Beanie. "Bob knew it, too, didn't he? He wanted to go to the cops, but you didn't. Because you're scared of the Gris brothers. Did they threaten you? The girls?"

Arms crossed, Belinda shook her head. "You don't know what you're talking about!"

"Belinda, let me help, okay," suggested Beanie. "Bob texted me the day he was shot because he wanted advice. I'm sure he wanted to know the best way to give the cops evidence that the Gris brothers—"

"Just a second," said Belinda, pulling a phone from her jacket pocket, staring at the screen. Frowning, she said, "I need to take this. And you need to leave. Now."

"Belinda …" Beanie called after her, but the designer ignored him as she hurried through the boutique and disappeared through an opening at the rear of the store.

Beanie exhaled. He knew he was right about the Gris brothers. He just had to get Belinda to trust him. He couldn't help her if she refused to come clean. Beanie knew she was worried about her daughters, afraid that the castoffs would go after them, concerned that she might face charges for whatever crimes the Gris brothers were forcing her to commit.

Determined to convince Belinda to do the right thing, Beanie walked toward the back of the boutique. He slipped into the opening and found himself in a small alcove. To the right was a door marked PRIVATE. To the left, a plaque with the word RESTROOM was mounted on the door. In front of him was a stockroom filled with clothes and boxes.

Beanie took a step toward the private office when he heard, "… supposed to get rid of the gun."

Belinda's voice, Beanie realized. Coming from the stockroom.

"It's a ghost gun," said a male voice, nasally and apathetic

"A ghost gun with my fucking prints on it," said Belinda. "A ghost gun with bullets that matched the bullet those doctors at St. Killian General took out of my husband's chest!"

"Cops ain't gonna be able to trace it," said the nasally guy. "Calm down."

"I would feel a lot better if the gun didn't exist."

"You want the gun gone, you get rid of it," said the guy. "I'm not getting in the middle of that beef with you and your husband."

"That beef between me and my husband had to be taken care of, Lanny," said Belinda. "And you know why."

Lanny? Beanie tensed. Had Belinda just called the guy Lanny? Could it be the same Lanny that Lime Shoes had told Beanie was a castoff working with Anna Zamora to sell drugs through the boutique? Beanie let out a slow breath and removed his phone from his pocket. Based on the topic of conversation, Belinda had to be talking to Lanny Gris.

"Couldn't have the love of my life ratting me out," said Belinda. "Couldn't have him telling the cops the truth about our operation."

"You're a cold-blooded bitch," said Lanny. "You shot your husband. Stabbed your business partner."

"I'm not proud of what I did," said Belinda. "But, I did what I had to … "

Beanie drug a hand down his face, scarcely able to believe what he was hearing. Fields was right. Belinda had shot Bob. And not only that, she'd stabbed Anna. Beanie didn't understand. He didn't know how to process what Belinda was saying. He just knew he had to let Officer Fields know what was happening.

Taking his phone from his pocket, he sent the policeman a text: *You were right. Belinda Davenport shot Bob. I overheard her say it. I'm at her boutique. She's with Lanny Gris.*

"You won't understand, Lanny, because you don't have kids," said Belinda, "but I have to think about my girls. They deserve everything I never had, and I'm going to make sure they want for nothing … and nothing will get in the way of that."

Minutes later, Fields texted: *Leave now! I'm headed there with back up!*

Beanie replied: *Ok.*

Lanny scoffed. "Nothing, huh? Not even the man you vowed to love, cherish, and obey, until death? Or, was that what you meant by until death do you part? Until you had to kill him?"

"He's not dead," Belinda snapped.

"Is that gonna be a problem?" asked Lanny.

"He's not going to rat me out," said Belinda. "He's got amnesia."

"Convenient," said Lanny, chuckling.

"Necessary," said Belinda. "If we're going to keep this operation going, then I have to keep Bob in line."

"Can you do that?"

"Bob knows I'll kill him if he doesn't keep his mouth shut," said Belinda.

Beanie pinched the bridge of his nose. Belinda had shot Bob to keep him quiet about her unauthorized operation with the Gris brothers. Bob must have found out, some way, that his wife wasn't the victim – she was the villain. Maybe that was why Bob wanted advice. Not on how to rat on the Gris brothers, but about how to betray his wife.

Sighing, Beanie turned.

His phone rang, a jaunty soca beat that looped over and over.

Beanie froze.

"What the hell was that?" asked Lanny. "Somebody out there?"

"Stay here," said Belinda. "I'll get rid of him."

Galvanized, Beanie headed out of the vestibule of the stockroom, and back onto the sales floor.

Fumbling the phone, Beanie glanced at the screen as he silenced the device. Noelle had been calling. No doubt, she'd arrived home, and when he wasn't there, she got worried and called to check on him. Beanie hated sending the call to voice mail, but once he left the boutique, he would call Noelle and—

"What are you still doing here?" Belinda asked, from behind him.

Beanie stopped. Cursing himself for not leaving when Fields had warned him, Beanie stared at the door. Fifteen more feet and he would have been out of the boutique. From a safe place across the street, he would have called his wife while he waited for Officer Fields and the cops to arrive and arrest Belinda Davenport and Lanny Gris.

Beanie took a breath and faced Belinda.

Standing about three feet away, the designer glared as she pointed a gun at him.

32

Beanie's stomach dropped, but he fought the panic threatening to engulf him.

Chaotic thoughts invaded his mind, trying to convince him that it was too late for him, that he wasn't going to survive, that he would die tonight. He struggled to silence the voices telling him that he should have answered the phone when Noelle called because he was never going to hear her voice again.

Beanie remembered the conversation he'd had with Octavia Constant, where he'd told her he would die for Noelle. And that was true. But, tonight, right now, he didn't want to die for Noelle. He wanted to live for his wife. And for his boys. He wanted more time with his family. Five years of marriage, four years with Ethan, and two years with Evan wasn't nearly enough. He wanted, no, he needed more time with his family. Whatever it took, he was going to go home to his family tonight.

"That necessary?" asked Beanie, indicating the gun with a slight tilt of his head.

"I think so," said Belinda. "Since I'm sure you overheard some things that you shouldn't have. Things you want to tell the cops and write about in the *Palmchat Gazette*."

Beanie fought the urge to turn around and run. Moments ago, when he'd been facing the door, he'd noticed there was no clear pathway to the exit. He'd have to zigzag through the shelves, display racks, and product tables positioned among fake potted palms and sitting areas where cane chairs, steamer trunks, and side tables were designed to mimic reading nooks.

If he remembered correctly, an immediate obstacle to his escape was a few feet behind him—a bamboo couch flanked by two four-foot bookshelves. If he pivoted and took off, he'd have to vault over the couch. Belinda might struggle to hit a moving target, but maybe not. Beanie couldn't take the chance. He would have to make a move, but it had to be the right move, not a hasty decision fueled by panic.

"I don't know what you think I heard, but—"

"I'm sure you heard me talking about how I killed Anna," said Belinda, the gun steady in her grip, trained on the center of his chest. "And how I shot Bob."

"Why'd you shoot him?" asked Beanie. He'd heard her reasons, but he needed to keep her talking and give himself time to survey his surroundings.

Sneering, Belinda said, "Bob was going to rat me out. Couldn't let that happen. Couldn't end up in jail. My girls need me."

Beanie held in a scoff. "Your girls need their father, too. You almost killed Bob. Your daughters would have been devastated."

"I shot Bob to scare him," said Belinda. "I knew he would survive. I know how to shoot someone without killing them. I was trained by some of the best Vadaj assassins to be a Disabler."

"A disabler?" asked Beanie, unfamiliar with the term, shifting his gaze to the right. About four feet away was a mannequin. Across from the mannequin was a wooden rack where colorful sundresses hung on bamboo hangers. Adjacent to the wooden rack was a display table. Further back was the cash wrap counter.

"A Disabler is someone who shoots to take you down, but not take you out," said Belinda. "Some people don't need to die. They just need to be disabled."

"You disabled Bob so he wouldn't go to the police?" asked Beanie, keeping his head still as he glanced to the left. A maze of gondola shelves, display tables, and another sitting area, behind which were two dressing rooms.

"When you disable a person," explained Belinda, "they go through a period of recovery, during which they will have time to reflect on their foolish decisions and actions, and most of the time, they'll see the error of their ways."

"And you're sure Bob has seen the error of his ways?" asked Beanie, thinking that he would go right, head to the cash wrap counter, and hide behind it. The counter, about six feet long and four feet high, would be a good barrier, protecting him until Fields and the cops arrived. Hopefully.

"My husband knows not to cross me," said Belinda.

"Was the amnesia his idea? Or yours?"

"I told Bob that he needed to forget some things he'd heard," said Belinda. "So, he told the cops he had amnesia."

"What did he hear?" asked Beanie, anxious to make a run for it, though he still wasn't sure about his decision. Hiding behind the cash wrap counter wouldn't put him closer to the exit, but he figured he'd be a sitting duck if he went for the door. Finding out that Belinda had pledged allegiance to the Vadaj family made the situation exponentially more dangerous.

"I was talking to Hugh Gris about how Anna wouldn't be a problem because I'd gotten rid of her," said Belinda. "I'd just finished my shower, and I had called Hugh and was talking to him. I'd thought Bob had gone to the kitchen, but he'd doubled back to join me in the shower. I didn't see Bob come in. When I ended the call and turned around, there he was, staring at me like I was some kind of monster."

"Maybe he was just in shock," suggested Beanie.

"Then he starts questioning me," said Belinda. "At first, I tried to pretend that I didn't know what he was talking about, but eventually, I just decided to come clean."

Beanie glanced right again. He would have to run between the mannequin and the rack of dresses, then skirt around the display table to get to the cash wrap counter.

"And then what happened?" Beanie asked.

Belinda shook her head. "He wants me to turn myself in. Can you believe that? I asked him, do you want me to go to jail for the rest of my life? Do you want me to miss out on seeing my girls grow up? He tells me I can say I accidentally killed Anna. That's crazy. As if it's possible to accidentally shove a knife in someone's chest?"

"What happened to Anna?" Beanie asked, hesitating. "How did you kill her?"

Shrugging, Belinda said, "Anna and Delaney left the house to go to the Hibiscus grove and have sex."

Beanie stared at Belinda. "What?"

"You didn't know about their affair?" asked Belinda, smirking. "Anna was the biggest slut in Avalon Estates. She screwed everybody. She strung Delaney along. They would hook up, and then Anna would kick her to the curb, sending Delaney into a murderous rage. That's why Delaney attacked Anna with those scissors. Wasn't because Anna had yelled at me, which she did. Delaney went after Anna because Anna had rejected her—again. But, soon, Anna called Delaney again for a secret midnight tryst in the Hibiscus bushes. Anna used to organize orgies in the Hibiscus grove. Everyone was invited. Bob and I never went, but Ernie, Victoria, Roger, and Ted, and a few other couples would engage. I'm surprised Florence didn't tell you about that ..."

Determined not to become distracting by the revelation, which might not have even been true, Beanie said, "And what happened after you followed Delaney and Anna?"

"After they hooked up," said Belinda, "they got into an argument. Anna said she didn't want to see Delaney anymore. Delaney told Anna that she was in love with her. It went on like that, ad nauseum. Until Delaney picked up a branch and whacked Anna with it. I was floored. So, Delaney runs off, and Anna is lying there, unconscious. And I thought, why not take advantage of the opportunity. So, I went back to the house, and got a knife from the kitchen. Anna was still unconscious in the hibiscus grove when I returned, and I stabbed her."

"And then you went back to the house a second time to find one of Ted's shirts to wrap the knife in?"

Belinda shrugged. "I needed someone to take the blame."

"You were going to frame Ted for Anna's murder?"

Again, Belinda lifted a shoulder.

Disturbed by the woman's ambivalence, Beanie asked, "So, you killed Anna because she was going to snitch on you to the PIIB?"

"Anna found out about the unauthorized operation," said Belinda. "At first, she was cool with it because of the money it was bringing in— money we needed. Then, she got worried because the cartel sent a representative to the boutique to tell her to shut down the operation because she didn't have permission to run it. I told her to let me handle things because I know how to deal with the PC-5, but she wouldn't listen. She called the PIIB, so ... she had to go. I wasn't about to go to jail because of that slutty bitch."

"You were willing to let Delaney go to jail for what you'd done?" asked Beanie.

"That whack job has so many screws loose that jail would probably do her some good," said Belinda. "Roger has her so doped up, she can hardly—"

Beanie pushed off his right foot, half-sprinting, half-sliding across the hardwood floor, heading right. A gunshot blasted as he dashed past the rack of dresses. Across from the dresses, the mannequin's head exploded, but Beanie kept going, diving around the display table, crouching as he heard another gunshot.

"What are you trying to prove?" asked Belinda. "You think you can outrun these bullets?"

Breathing heavily, Beanie tried to discern Belinda's position without rising and exposing his head, which she would no doubt take aim at. With the echo of shots ringing in his ears and the smell of Cordite singeing his nostrils, it was hard to hear her footsteps. Was she to the left of him? Or, to the right?

"Don't bother running around trying to dodge bullets," said Belinda. "I'm going to shoot you. And when I do, you'll be dead. Not disabled."

Pivoting on his heels, Beanie faced the cash wrap counter, three feet away. Could he make it? He wasn't sure, but he had to try. If he had to dodge bullets to make it home to his family, he would.

Senses heightened, Beanie did a rolling dive from the display to the cash wrap counter, bullets following him. Scrambling behind the cash wrap, he flattened himself against the floor, and—

"Drop the gun, Mrs. Davenport!" Came the terse command, followed by the heavy footsteps on the hardwood floor. "Put your hands up and—"

More gunshots, a series of popping blasts that seemed to Beanie to go on forever. Huddled behind the cash wrap counter, Beanie prayed he wouldn't be the victim of a wayward bullet. Finally, the gunshots stopped after a shrieking howl reverberated throughout the store. There was a loud, clanging thud.

"On your knees!"

"I'm shot, you son of a bitch!" Belinda cursed.

"Cuff her!" the terse order came from a familiar voice—Officer Damon Fields.

Flooded with relief, Beanie announced his position and asked for permission to stand. Seconds later, Officer Fields stood in front of him. "What the hell are you still doing here? Thought I told you to leave."

Rising to his feet, Beanie leaned against the counter, his legs wobbly. "I should have listened to you."

Shaking his head, Officer Fields asked, "You okay? You hit?"

"I'm okay," said Beanie, and smiled, knowing that he would be going home to his family.

EPILOGUE

"Bob took my advice," said Beanie, adjusting the pillows behind his head.

A week had passed since the shootout at the boutique.

"He's going to testify against Belinda?" asked Noelle, walking toward their king-sized bed.

"He said it's the right thing to do," said Beanie. "Still, I know it's going to be hard for him. He loves Belinda and doesn't want to see her in prison, but he's got to think of the girls."

"Belinda wasn't," said Noelle. "I can't believe she was working with PC-5 castoffs."

"Unfortunately, those castoffs got away," said Beanie. "The cops think Lanny snuck out of the boutique before they showed up. He and his brother Hugh probably fled the island. Police have no idea where they are."

Noelle shook her head. "I still can't believe that Belinda fooled everybody. She was actually selling drugs out of the boutique."

Beanie said, "Belinda claims she was trafficking narcotics so her girls could have a better life."

"She put her daughters' lives in danger," said Noelle. "An unauthorized operation is dangerous enough, and she had to make it worse by working with the Gris brothers. She made herself and her entire family a target."

As his wife stretched out next to him, Beanie said, "With Belinda in prison, Bob and the girls won't have to worry about the PC-5."

Noelle said, "I know, but, it's heartbreaking because the girls are losing their mother and for what? Greed. Money."

Beanie sighed. The situation was complicated and sad. He wasn't quite sure how to feel or what to think about everything that happened. On the one hand, he was relieved that the murder of Anna Zamora and Bob's attempted murder had been solved. Belinda was in jail, having been denied bond, awaiting trial for her crimes, which included illegal drug trafficking.

On the other hand, after talking to Bob Davenport yesterday, Beanie felt sorry for the man. Belinda's crimes had crushed Bob. A broken man, he was resolved to make sure justice was served, but Beanie wasn't sure the stay-at-home dad would ever recover from his wife's brutal betrayal. Beanie could only hope that Bob would center his life around his daughters and allow the unconditional love of his girls to heal his shattered heart.

"I'm just glad that the charges against Delaney were dropped and she's getting the help she needs. I think some time at the Rakestraw-Blake Center would be good for her," said Beanie. "Better than Roger, who I suspect was over medicating her."

Noelle nodded. "Well, even though nothing feels like it will ever be normal, things seem to be getting back to normal. Ted is back at work. Ernie and Victoria are doing fine. And Florence and Chuck are still gossiping about everyone in Avalon Estates."

Beanie exhaled. "Babe, that place."

"I know," said Noelle. "So many secrets and craziness and lies."

"I used to want to live in that neighborhood," confessed Beanie. "When I was in high school, I had a paper route. I would ride my bicycle up and down those palm-lined streets and dream about buying one of those million dollar mansions, but now, you couldn't pay me to live there."

Snuggling closer to him, Noelle asked, "Not even if you could participate in those midnight orgies in the hibiscus grove?"

Beanie pulled Noelle on top of him. "What do I need an orgy for? I have you ..."

Message from Rachel ...

Did you figure out who murdered Anna before Beanie did?

There were a lot of suspects and even more sinister secrets to uncover but once Beanie figured out the devious motives of the people who wanted Anna dead, he figured out the killer.

As an investigative reporter, Beanie always finds himself dealing with a dead body, especially around a holiday.

Easter brought a corpse beneath a Hibiscus bush.

Christmas, that festive time where it's better to give than to receive, brings more mayhem when Beanie and his boys witness a vicious attack on Santa Claus!

In MERRY CHRISTMAS MURDER, you'll have to figure out ...

Who shot Old St. Nick?

Investigative reporter Roland "Beanie" Bean uncovers a strange connection between a gunshot victim and the attempted murder of a man who played Santa Claus at a mall. But discovering the truth will force him to face a ruthless killer determined to make sure the truth stays hidden.

MERRY CHRISTMAS MURDER is a contemporary whodunit murder mystery novel.

Grab your copy of MERRY CHRISTMAS MURDER now!

https://amzn.to/3zaPgnl

EXCLUSIVE OFFER

Rachel Woods entertains readers with her riveting mysteries, from cozies to whodunits. Now you can get one of her books for FREE, when you sign up to join her newsletter:

GET MY FREE BOOK NOW

https://BookHip.com/HJQQCKN

ALSO BY RACHEL WOODS

REPORTER ROLAND BEAN COZY MYSTERIES

Roland "Beanie" Bean, husband and loving father, finds himself the unwitting participant in solving crimes as he seeks to make a name for himself as a reporter for the *Palmchat Gazette*.

EASTER EGG HUNT MURDER

MERRY CHRISTMAS MURDER

TRICK OR TREAT MURDER

GOBBLE GOBBLE MURDER

PALMCHAT ISLANDS MYSTERIES

Married journalists, Vivian and Leo, manage the island newspaper while solving crimes as they chase leads for their next story.

UNTIL DEATH DO US PART

NO ONE WILL FIND YOU

YOU WILL DIE FOR THIS

DON'T MAKE ME HURT YOU

THE PALMCHAT ISLANDS MYSTERIES BOX SET: BOOKS 1 - 4

SPENCER & SIONE SERIES

Gripping romantic suspense series with steamy romance, unpredictable plot twists and devastating consequences of deceit.

HER DEADLY MISTAKE

HER DEADLY DECEPTION

HER DEADLY THREAT

HER DEADLY BETRAYAL

HER DEADLY ENCOUNTER

THE SPENCER & SIONE SERIES BOX SET: BOOKS 1 - 5

MURDER IN PARADISE SERIES

A series of stand-alone women sleuth mysteries with murder, mayhem and a dash of romance, set against the backdrop of turquoise waters and swaying palm trees of the fictional Palmchat Islands.

THE UNWORTHY WIFE

THE PERFECT LIAR

THE SILENT ENEMY

ABOUT THE AUTHOR

Rachel Woods studied journalism and graduated from the University of Houston where she published articles in the Daily Cougar. She is a legal assistant by day and a freelance writer and blogger with a penchant for melodrama by night. Many of her stories take place on the islands, which she has visited around the world. Rachel resides in Houston, Texas with her three sock monkeys.

For more information:
www.therachelwoods.com
rachel@therachelwoods.com

facebook.com/therachelwoodsauthor
instagram.com/therachelwoodsauthor
bookbub.com/authors/rachel-woods
amazon.com/author/therachelwoods

ABOUT THE PUBLISHER

BONZAIMOON BOOKS

BonzaiMoon Books is a family-run, artisanal publishing company created in the summer of 2014. We publish works of fiction in various genres. Our passion and focus is working with authors who write the books you want to read, and giving those authors the opportunity to have more direct input in the publishing of their work.

For more information:
www.bonzaimoonbooks.com
info@bonzaimoonbooks.com

facebook.com/BonzaiMoonBooks
twitter.com/bonzaimoon

Printed in Great Britain
by Amazon

78641361R00091